WITH HER MAJESTY'S SECRET CORGIS

rene fomby

Book Ness
Monster
Press

Book Ness Monster Press
4530 Blue Ridge Drive
Belton, Texas 76513

Copyright © 2020 by Rene Fomby.
Paperback ISBN: 978-1-947304-12-3

Visit us on the World Wide Web: http://www.renefomby.com

Fomby, Rene. With Her Majesty's Secret Corgis.
Book Ness Monster Press. Paperback Edition.

To Dirk and Spot

London

S he glided effortlessly down the empty hall, nose held high in the air, her quick steps clattering noisily against the cold stone walls of the palace. With the Queen off at Windsor for the week, much of the palace staff had taken advantage of her absence to go on holiday themselves, leaving the castle desperately undermanned. And quite vulnerable, don't you know.

But Ginger would have none of that. With the Queen away, that only meant the opportunity for mischief was doubled, making her job as head of the Secret Service even more difficult. If only she could teach her underlings to be as fastidious about their duties. But the youngsters they were hiring these days—bah!—no work ethic whatsoever. Just show up, put in the hours, then off to play like a carefree pack of unweaned puppies. Well, nothing she could do about that. Except set an example, she supposed. Show them every single day what it would take to make top dog around here.

Ginger had worked almost nonstop to get to where she was today, quite literally turning over almost every stone she passed along the way lest they conceal some venomous snake or insect that could threaten the Palace's tenants. As Chief of Station for Her Majesty's Secret Service, she reported directly to none other than M, herself head of PETSEC's United Kingdom operation and, other than the Queen, perhaps the most powerful female in all of England. Under M, PETSEC UK had grown from a sleepy backwater office to now head of the international pet security organization's global intelligence operations, including the secretive yet infamous Double-O stable of spies and killer agents. Second only to PETSEC's worldwide headquarters in Chicago—the city where the organization was founded in the chaos following the Great War—the UK branch had grown to eclipse even the EU offices in Brussels, of which it was still technically only a member state, equal in stature to all of the other countries of Europe.

As Chief of Station, Ginger's responsibilities included the protection of every member of the Royal Family, and every single one of their far-flung castles and palaces and manors. But of course, none of those Royals was more important than her Queen, and consequently no palace presented a greater risk to her monarch than this one, the Queen's primary residence. A risk that grew greater every day, as the old protocols and observances that had maintained order, dignity and—most important of all—a reasonable measure of respectful distance between her wards and the unpolished and untrustworthy masses that pressed in on them so threateningly each and every day. Well, there was nothing she could do about that little problem except redouble her efforts to keep the Queen and family safe from harm—and keep the unwashed public at bay.

Putting those dark thoughts behind her, she waddled into the next hall, and the cluster of servants standing huddled together near the doorway (trading what was almost certainly cheap and malicious gossip) took one long look at her trademark russet mane and immediately found something better to do. She made a quick note of their names for her report at the end of the day. With the Queen away, the mice will play. Well, she'd certainly see about that!

A noise from close behind startled her, and she spun around quickly to see who was following her, but before she could make the turn completely she was swallowed up whole dog in a large and somewhat furry black sack. And then everything went completely black as well.

But not before she got a good long whiff of a very familiar old scent. Beets.

Bella

Limehouse Marina, London

A heavy fog is hanging dripping wet over the water slapping against the side of our boat just outside the kitchen window as I check my food bowl for the third time this morning. Drat, still empty! And Moose's is empty, too! My stomach is growling in protest like a bear coming out of a long hibernation, but there is nothing I can do about until Helen returns from whatever random Sunday morning errand she has run off to handle. At least the water bowl is on autofill, so maybe I can fill up for the time being on that.

As for Moose, after breakfast he pushed his black stubby nose through our doggie door and is now stretched out on the prow of our little barge, sunning himself like he doesn't have a care in the world. Which I have to admit he mostly doesn't.

The trip from Chicago to London was mostly pretty uneventful for us. Helen pulled some strings somehow and managed for Moose and I to fly in the main cabin rather than be stuffed down in the cold dark hold like long forgotten baggage. Part of that was probably due to the upgrade to first class, which

Howard grumbled about almost nonstop, but finally caved in under a sharp and unrelenting barrage from Helen. But however that little miracle happened, I am forever grateful for it. I had a chocolate Lab friend back in Chicago who traveled in baggage once, and the stories she told about the experience were quite frightening, indeed. Drugged to the gills, then tossed about from here to there willy nilly like some kind of animal. An absolutely in-canine solution, if you ask me!

Knowing deep in my heart the food bowl isn't going to somehow get filled back up all by itself, despite what my stomach keeps telling me, I pick out a soft and sunny spot on the couch in the salon and have just settled in for a well deserved nap when suddenly I hear voices coming from the front of the boat. Having had lots of experience with the kind of trouble Moose can get himself into when he's left unsupervised, I bounce down off the sofa and trot forward to check it all out.

Coming through the doggie door, I catch Moose engaged in earnest conversation with some strange dog I've never seen before at the marina. He looks an awful lot like Moose, other than being slightly smaller in stature, if that is even possible. He's wearing a garishly bright sweater and some kind of floppy gray cap. Oh, and did I mention that he seems to be missing one eye, his right? Not exactly something you come across every day.

"I say," says the strange dog, giving me the one eye. "What have we here? You've been holding out on me, Moose! And she's quite the looker, I'll give you that."

"Excuse me?" I am completely floored and more than a little offended by his arrogant remarks, even if they did sound a little less offensive spoken as they were in his soft, burring English accent. Or, since he's apparently an Australian Terrier like Moose, is it an Aussie accent? Being an American and having very little experience dealing with such things, I find it's really hard to tell the difference. But since we're in England, after all, it's a safe bet it's probably English. British English, that is. Not the real American kind.

"Sorry, ma'am," the dog adds, immediately doffing the small cap he has perched on the very top of his head. "Allow me to introduce meself. The name is Patton, Patton Mountbatten, to be precise. And you must be Bella."

That surprises me to no end. Did Moose offer up my name to this stranger without asking me first? Or is it that this odd fellow and I have a mutual friend somewhere? "How—"

"Sorry again, ma'am. But as I was just telling your friend here, I'm not exactly here on a social visit. I've been sent here to retrieve the two of you."

"Sent here? By whom?" I must tell you, I am not at all comfortable with the notion of heading off into this strange and dangerous city, towing behind an even stranger dog. And one with only one eye at that. Sure, Moose has been known to run off barking at shadows at the drop of a hat, but at the mere doff of a hat? No way, not this girl.

"Why, I've been sent by the Palace, my lady. Something's happened there. They won't tell me exactly what it is, at least not over an unsecured line, but they made it clear the two of you are needed there quite desperately. So they sent me along to find you."

I glance over at Moose, who just shrugs his shoulders. Evidently he is every bit as lost here as I am. "What palace? And again, who exactly has the overbearing gall to think I should come running just because they say so. It's nappy time, you know…"

"Yes, my lady," Patton replies, lowering his gaze a bit. "But I'm sure they wouldn't have sent for you if it wasn't some kind of dire emergency. Especially since the two of you are…" His voice drops off slightly. "Colonists."

Colonists? Why, what kind of arrogant English snobbery… "Harrumph! I'll have you know we are both proud, loyal citizens of the United States of America, and we whipped your country's behind not once but twice to establish that claim. And by gosh we'll do it all over once again if we ever need to. So there!"

It's obvious my words have stung him deeply, but still the one-eyed dog persists. "Yes, my lady, I understand. But still… the summons?"

"Yes, the summons." I see Moose giving me the look, the one he uses on me whenever he thinks I'm taking things a bit over the top, so I decide to let it go for the moment. At least until I find out what this is all about.

"Okay, Mr. Patton, let me ask you one last time. Just who is it that wants to see us? And why?" I pointedly refuse to give this blowhard the honor of calling him by his last name.

With the change in my tone, he seems to straighten up just a bit, and flashes me a quick if crooked smile. "Why, it's Her Majesty's Secret Service, my dear lady. At Barkingham Palace."

Outside Barkingham Palace

B eing that I'm used to having a driver anytime I need to get anywhere, anywhere at all, I'll have to tell you the trip to the palace was quite long and arduous, involving jumping on and off noisy human trains both high above the ground and a disturbing distance below it, followed by a seemingly endless walkie through a patch of pond, grass and flowers that Patton called St. James's Park. Moose has managed to sneeze the entire way through the park, while I just stay focused on keeping a wary eye on all the squirrels and the waterfowl, in particular one spindly-legged bird with an oversized beak that appears to be following us at a distance, ducking behind trees and bushes every time I look back. You just never know where the next threat is going to come from when you're traveling in foreign lands.

"I'm sorry, Bella," Moose is explaining to me apologetically in between sneezes, his right forearm now almost totally covered in the green slimy evidence of his condition. "I—I guess I'm just allergic to all the flowers. I had a similar problem back when I was a puppy, but at some point Helen got rid of all the natural flowers in the house and planted silk ones instead. I don't seem to mind silk flowers for some reason. Plus they last a whole lot longer, so I fail to really understand why anyone would want the other kind, you know?"

I don't really have the time or energy to explain to him that silk flowers aren't real, that they're made up out of caterpillar poop. Or something like that, pretty gross when you really think about it. But now that I do think about it, unlike my previous mistress who just loved blowing money on fresh bouquets of flowers every few days or so, I've never seen any real flowers in my new home, neither here in London nor during the few weeks I stayed at Moose's house back in Chicago. Helen must not like them for some reason. Odd.

Oh well, despite all of Moose's sneezing and wheezing we finally manage to find our way to the front of the palace. Moose is apparently so taken aback by the sheer size of the place he's wandered slack-jawed straight into the street, right out in front of a long line of human men riding these absolutely massive horses, both horses and men alike covered from head to hoof with all kinds of jackets and whatnot to the point where it's almost impossible to tell where the horses end and the humans begin. Anyway, like I said, Moose being Moose and all, he would have been smashed flat by one of those horses' enormous hooves if Patton hadn't seized him by the collar and pulled him back out of the way at the very last minute. And by the way, I couldn't help but notice how he grabbed him by some kind of weird, space-age looking blue collar, with tiny blinking lights and an almost metallic sheen to it. Strange that I hadn't noticed that before.

Anyway, with Moose now safely ensconced at the curb, well out of the way, Patton is pointing a paw toward the left side of the palace—our left, that is— where a small road filled with human tourists borders the stone walls surrounding the complex. "Over there. The Barkingham Mews gift shop. That's our entrance to the palace."

We quickly make our way across the street, all the while studiously dodging the throngs of tourists and any stray horses or other beasts that might be stomping dangerously in our direction, and soon find our way to the front of the gift shop. Patton stops and waves his muzzle toward the door.

"Okay, laddies and lassies, here's the thing. The gift shop staff is used to my coming and going, and as for Bella, they'll just see her as one of the Queen's Corgis, out for a morning constitutional. An everyday occurrence around these parts. Moose, on the other paw, might draw some unwanted attention, so we just need to hitch up our haunches and march in there with our muzzles held up high like we own the place— which in fact we pretty much do—and then head straight for the back. The key is, no eye contact, get it? They've all been trained to look the other way as far as we're concerned, so unless you draw attention to yourself, we should get through the shop safely with no real trouble. Think you two can manage that?"

I find his whole condescending attitude rather offensive, talking to us like we're nothing more than a bunch of puppies fresh out of the litter, but I nod for him to lead the way. Moose, for his part, is mostly nonresponsive up to this point, simply gawking at everything he passes with his eyes bulging out and his jaw hanging wide open. Which, to be fair, is pretty much his go-to look these days. I would've left him back on the boat, snoozing away the rest of the morning, but then there's no telling what disaster that

16

might have caused. And I have a long list of quite telling examples on that particular topic, believe you me.

Anyway, as we duck through the doorway into the tiny gift shop, I can see immediately that Patton was dead right about the humans. I mean, we're three random dogs trotting in from off the street with not a master or mistress anywhere to be found, and instead of shooing us all outside, which I would have expected under any normal circumstances, all of the shop staff seem to have suddenly found something vitally important to busy themselves with, whether it's straightening up a shelf of royalty-related knickknacks or recounting the money in the till or simply staring straight up at the ceiling, like they're searching for spiderwebs or something. Anything other than looking our way. Odd. Very odd.

Patton doesn't seem in all that much of a hurry as he dodges between the legs of various tourists oohing and aahing over dishtowels and Christmas ornaments and teacups with the Queen's seal on the front, and simply trots nonchalantly toward the door leading to the back of the shop. Moose and I follow close behind, and in that order. Moose, then me. I can't

17

risk letting Moose fall behind me—if ever there was a dog that needed herding, it would be that one. And, as you almost certainly are fully aware, we Corgis were originally bred for herding. It's what we do best. Other than licking. Oh, yeah, and barking. Can't forget that.

Anyway, once inside the back room our trip becomes a dark, confusing maze of secret panels and corridors, until we finally push through the fanciest doggie door I've ever seen and step out into a room that the word opulent can't possibly hope to describe. In fact, I don't think Standard American Doglish even has a vocabulary to describe the kind of garish, over-the-top spectacle that is laid out in front of me like some kind of human version of a big-box pet store. I mean, there are pictures of dead humans covering almost every inch of the walls! Massive pictures, and all apparently painted by hand, like the ones Helen painted and had hanging on the walls in our house back in Chicago, only these actually look real. Oh, and the gold! There is gold covering almost every single surface in the room that isn't painted, and it's shining so bright I have to squint my eyes for a moment before they finally adjust and I can look around without holding up a paw to block it.

I look down and find myself standing on a carpet that feels softer underfoot than the pillows on Helen's couch, and when I take a closer look I see that my paws have almost disappeared down into it, the deep blue tufts of supple wool rising up over my knuckles, sucking them in and making it a little hard to walk, like that one time my old mistress took me to that hot sandy beach in Indiana. Ah, a nice memory, it was, even if my mistress turned out to be not so really nice. Okay, really not nice at all, to be entirely honest, like that cruel lady that tried to off all those Dalmatians in the movie. Luckily, like the Dalmatians, everything worked out well for me in the end, so I guess I should be grateful.

Anyway, back to the carpet, I glance over at Moose, and he seems to be having the same problem I'm struggling with, picking up his left paw and then setting it back down, then testing the carpet tentatively with his right paw. As if that's going to make any kind of a difference. It's just a weird sensation, I'll have to tell you, but I guess we just need to adjust to it. Kind of like everything else we've experienced since we landed in this crazy country.

A sharp woof from somewhere down the hall catches my attention, and I look up to see Patton patting the ground as well, but judging from the impatient look on his face he doesn't seem all that interested in the carpet or the paintings.

"Are you going to stand there all day, sniffing around?" he growls at me. "We have a bloody meeting to attend, I tell you, and we're late! Come along, ruddychop-chop!"

I give Moose a sideways look that speaks volumes about what I think of old mister one-eye, but the two of us take off after him anyway, veering off the carpet to make better time on the hardwood floors along the edge. It means we have to dodge a few chair legs and side tables every now and then, but it's well worth it as we scurry off down the hall and through another confusing set of twists and turns, passing room after room, doorway after doorway, with nothing more to guide us than Patton's squat little brown tail, somehow staying well ahead of us no matter how hard we trot. Every now and then I have to give Moose a gentle nip on his own brown Aussie rump to keep him focused on staying up with us, his tiny terrier brain drifting off every time we pass a bowl of fruit or a houseplant that looks like it might be marked up with an interesting pee-mail or two that he somehow needs to answer right away.

Finally, Patton comes to a halt in a large, cavernous room with plush red velvet walls that seem to rise up forever to a towering ceiling lined down the middle with several ginormous crystal chandeliers. My eyes are still sparkling from the light of what must be a million jewels when I finally look down and see that another dog has joined us. A Pembroke, just like me. Well, when I say just like me, I really mean she is nothing at all like me, other than being a girl, of course. And, like I said, a Pembroke Welsh Corgi. But otherwise, we are every bit as different as night and day.

Out of the corner of my eye I see Moose cocking his head in surprise. "Hey, Bella, you didn't tell me you had an identical twin sister. And all the way over in England, at that. How in the world did you pull that off?"

"What do you mean, identical?" I spit at him indignantly under my breath. "Why, we're nothing at all alike. Just look at her! That white stripe down the top of her nose, it's way thicker than mine. Her nails are all rounded off at the end, instead of cut straight across like they should be. And she doesn't even have a tail! Honestly, Moose, sometimes I don't think you pay a bit of attention to all the important details right in front of your nose. It amazes me you can even find your way to your water bowl…"

While I'm busy correcting Moose, the new dog is just standing there watching us with an amused looking smile smeared across her face. Or at least I think it's a smile. We Corgis just naturally have mouths on us that seem to turn up a bit at the ends, so sometimes it's hard to tell for sure. But Patton is most assuredly not smiling, and he's starting to creep me out a little, staring at us with that one unblinking eye of his.

And then I do a double-take. Somewhere along the way he's changed outfits! Instead of the ugly sweater and cap combination, now he's wearing a black velvet smoking jacket and a tall shiny top hat. And he's sporting a gold monocle over his one eye!

Patton must have noticed my reaction because he quickly gives us a small bow, doffing his hat for a moment before straightening up and resetting it on top of his head, his ears sprouting up out of small holes on either side of the brim. He smiles at us, and being in this fancy palace and all, I'm expecting to see a perfect row of brilliant white choppers, but instead his teeth are all topsy turvy and more than a little in need of cleaning, like a box of Chiclets that have been run over by a semi truck. "Ah, you've noticed I've changed my attire, put on something more suited to the occasion," he says in an accent that has jumped more than a few social levels up from how he sounded earlier today back on the boat.

I don't say anything at first, but just nod my muzzle up and down like some kind of village idiot, still trying to process everything that is going on.

One-Eye continues. "Well, unfortunately I've become quite well known around London over the years, and it wouldn't do to head out of the Palace on a secret mission without donning some type of disguise, now would it?"

"Uh, no," I agree, still feeling a little off my paws by the velvet jacket and that hat, not the sort of thing I'd ever thought I'd see a dog wearing, not even a purse doggie like this one. I decide to break the awkwardness of the situation by introducing myself to the Pembroke. "Hi, I'm Bella. Bella—uh, McGillicutty. And this here is Moose." I'm still not

23

used to my new last name, the name I adopted when I joined Moose's family a few months back. My old name was Smith, which you'll have to admit is much simpler and kind of rolls off the tongue better when you say it. But McGillicutty isn't all that bad, really. Especially since, like I said, it makes me a part of Moose's family. His sister, in fact. But then I suddenly realize I've been going on and on, not paying attention, and the other Corgi is saying something—

"...good of you to come. We've had a spot of bother around here today, and we're rather shorthanded, the Queen being at Windsor and all that, so we greatly appreciate your taking the time to help us out." Not-Twin pronounces the word "schedules" like it starts with "shed", and that throws me for a second. She takes in my quizzical expression and evidently misreads it to mean something else. Something other than my complete confusion over what in the world is going on around here. She holds up a paw and waves it slightly, more like a twist, really, and on the other side of the room a human I hadn't noticed before bows and breaks into a brisk run down the hall. "How boorish of me. Where are my manners!" she says, cocking her head ever so slightly. "You must be feeling frightfully peckish, having traveled all this way over from the East End. I knew I should have sent a driver, what was I thinking? Here, dear, do sit a spell while the butler brings us a spot of tea."

She squats down on her haunches and Patton quickly joins her. It takes me a second to make sure I have my hind legs arranged in the proper fashion, mimicking the two of them, but then I sit, as well. Moose is still looking around starry-eyed—big surprise there—so I give him a soft, telling woof and point one paw toward the floor. He hesitates, looking first at me and then the floor, then seems to finally get the picture of what is happening and plops down himself.

In less than a minute the butler returns, carrying a silver tray bearing four small bowls of sparkling water and a platter heaped full with delicious-looking biscuits. Proper dog biscuits, that is, not the kind Helen eats with all that nasty white gravy poured all on top. Moose makes a move like he is going for the biscuits straight up just as soon as they're laid in front of us, but I manage to hold him back with one short wave of my paw. It wouldn't do for us to look like some kind of uneducated country bumpkins, not here on our very first visit to the palace. End up giving this odd-looking British Corgi and Old One-Eye the wrong impression of our upbringing. But then I remember, Moose is an Aussie, not a refined canine like the rest of us, so I suppose some of that coarseness of breeding is to be expected.

The Palace Pembroke is speaking again, her thick English accent making it rather difficult for me to follow along.

"As I said, with Ginger now amiss, we're in a bit of a pickle here at the Palace. It isn't at all like her to simply up and vanish like that, leave without a trace or a simple polite note to tell us where she's gone off to. And with Her Majesty expected back at the Palace in just two days' time, it wouldn't do to have her return and find out that her favorite Corgi is in the wind like that. It wouldn't do at all!"

She says it like I'm supposed to understand why, and Patton is nodding along. I look over at Moose, who seems to have stretched out on the soft carpet while the Corgi had my full attention, and is now nodding off. I pick up a bit of a biscuit and bounce it off his nose, getting his full attention.

"Wha—" he sputters, sitting back up. I decide to use his lack of attention to full advantage.

"I am so very sorry," I say, covering for him, "but my friend Moose here had a rough go of it last night and didn't get a wink of sleep, so he's feeling a bit out of it, I'm afraid. But I do so want him to be in on everything that's going on here. Would you mind repeating all of what you just explained for his benefit?"

Pembroke Not-Twin gives me a look that says she does very much mind, says it in volumes, but after rolling her eyes she turns to Moose and starts over. Or at least I think it's from the start. Like I said, I wasn't really paying all that much attention at the time.

"As I was saying, Lord Mountbatten here is the founder of Her Majesty's Secret Service at the palace. His family is quite famous, you know, having won the war and all that."

Moose has latched onto a large biscuit and is chewing intently on it as he listens, crumbs dropping at his feet. "Oh yeah! I thought I heard that name before, back from when I was in obedience school. He was that great war hero, a general, if I remember right, General—"

Not-Twin is nodding enthusiastically at that. "Yes. That is correct. General—"

"Patton," Moose crows, smiling widely at having gotten it right for a change.

Not-Twin's smile droops. "Uh, no, not Patton. Mountbatten, actually," she says, her chirpy British tone sliding down a notch. "The general's name was Mountbatten. Part of the royal family, you know."

Moose shakes his head, and biscuit particles fly everywhere. "No, no, I'm pretty sure it was General Patton. Well, anyway, any relative of the good general is a friend of mine. Put it there!"

Moose sticks out a paw in One-Eye's direction, and after a long awkward moment during which One-Eye makes no indication that he plans to respond in kind, he pulls it back.

"Oh, I see. Never learned to shake, is that it?" Moose says with a grin. "Well, we can't all be college educated, I guess." He turns back to face Not-Twin, the biscuit now fully consumed. "So, babe, how about you? You got a name?" he asks, squinting to see if she is wearing a tag of some sort on her collar. Which she is not. That may be some kind of English thing, I don't know, but it seems to me having a name tag is pretty fundamental as far as manners go. And not having a rabies tag? That's just screaming that you don't give a hoot about public health, at least as far as I'm concerned.

Evidently tagless Not-Twin has now dropped some of her high-and-mightiness and is speaking again, the scowl on her face not doing her aging appearance any favors.

"—my name is Victoria, like the queen. Now that Lord Mountbatten has semi-retired, I am the Secretary to her lady Ginger, and therefore second in command of Her Majesty's Secret Service. And currently first in command, I suppose, given Ginger's inexplicable absence."

I decide that now is a great time to interrupt and fill in a few blanks. "Uh, okay, for Moose's sake, can you go over all that about Ginger again? I think he missed most of it the first time."

Moose is giving me a look like I'm speaking absolute cat gibberish, like when the humans try out all that insulting baby talk on us, but Queen Victoria or whatever is busy happily rehashing the whole Ginger story.

"So, as I explained before, Ginger came to the Palace as a pup, barely weaned. She was an orphan, her mother having unfortunately been crushed by a speeding lorry in the streets of Bath, and like most of the Corgis coming out of Bath she was born a ginger. A red-head. Hence the name the Queen bestowed upon her when she first arrived. Being a pup, though, not much was expected of her, particularly since she had been born sickly, the runt of the litter. That was why they never docked her tail, which is by the way a most ghastly and completely in-canine practice that has now been banned everywhere within the UK. Thanks almost entirely to the dogged efforts of PETSEC EU, lobbying Parliament for recognition of the most fundamental rights of dogs and cats throughout our Kingdom."

Not-Me suddenly stops and catches my eye, pointing toward my rear end with a knowing look. "And that, by the way, is one of the reasons we summoned you here today. Your tail. There just aren't very many Corgis on the Island your age that haven't been docked, and even Q'ute Branch hasn't found a way to throw together a robotic prosthetic tail that actually looks completely authentic. Although they're hard at work on it, for sure. It's only a matter of time, you understand."

At the mention of Q'ute Branch, Moose's ears perk up again. "You know Q'ute?" he asks. "Is she here in England? I'd love to see her again. We—uh—we kinda had this—thing going on, you might call it. Back in Chicago."

Victoria gives him a fiercely skeptical look, then continues on, her scowl if anything growing even deeper. "Anyway, Ginger had just arrived at the Palace and was still getting her bearings—as you may have noticed, the Palace is quite large, and it is quite easy to get lost in here, even with our keen sense of smell—when Daniel Craig came to film the opening sequence for the London Olympics. As you no doubt recall, he was reprising his iconic role as Agent 007, James Bond, and escorting Her Majesty into a helo to whisk her off to the opening ceremony—"

Moose can't help but butt in again. "Oh, I know 007. Well, I mean, I met the sharks that ate him, at the Shedd Aquarium back in Chicago. My take was he was kind of a bit player at the time, if you know what I mean, heh heh. Get it? *Bit* player?"

Victoria gives off a look like she's just been slapped, but still manages to soldier on. "As I was saying, the scene was completed on schedule, but the next morning we got a call that for some reason the video had been corrupted and needed to be reshot. I must give our Queen due credit, she had a full calendar on tap that day, particularly given her age, but nevertheless she agreed without hesitation to squeeze in a reshoot. All for her country, you must understand. For our Queen, crown and country comes above all else. One reason we Corgis are all willing to lay down our lives in her defense."

"Whoa," Moose sputters again. "I mean, I get the part that she's the queen and all, but she's getting up to like, what, almost twenty in dog years? At some point you've just got to be willing to pull the plug on the old girl, you know? There's got to be some younger pups down the line that are more than eager to put on the collar, you know what I mean?"

Victoria is now looking for all the world like she's swallowed a rancid mouthful of kibble and can't find a place to spit it out. "My dear Moose, it's a *crown*, not a collar. And no, it doesn't work like that. We have but one Monarch in the United Kingdom, and whatever happens, we must do everything in our power to preserve and protect her. Even if it means sacrificing ourselves in the process."

Moose is still quite obviously unconvinced. "Yeah, well, where I come from, that seems like a moron's move. The guy we pick, we get a chance every four years to kick the boob out of office. And after eight years, regardless of what's going on, the guy gets sent out on the gin and rubber chicken circuit to finally make his millions, selling bankrupt insights to well-heeled audiences who should know better than to shell out ten thousand bucks for a meal. A meal they could buy better and much cheaper at a KFC, in my humble canine opinion."

Victoria Not-Twin has drawn herself back up to full-on haughty status, and with a knowing glance in the direction of One-Eye continues. "Be that as it may, the point is, even as a mere pup Ginger made it abundantly clear she was something special."

"Oh, you mean Special Ed?" Moose asks enthusiastically, ignoring my every effort to try and get him to pipe down for a change. He never did know when to shut up. "Yeah, I knew a Golden Retriever like that once. Couldn't even find her way back home if she didn't have this Jack Russell tailing her the whole time to make sure she was okay. I remember this one time—"

Victoria interrupts him with a loud *harrumph*. "No, not special education, Mr. Moose. *Special*," she intones weightily, eyeing One-Eye somewhat plaintively for support. He nods and takes over for her. A bit reluctantly, it seems to me, and that unblinking eye of his is still creeping me out.

"I was there when the film crew arrived on the second day," he snips in his clipped little Aussie/English accent. "The Bond fellow, of course, and several others with cameras and lights. We started the filming in the Queen's private office, then moved down the hall toward the helo. Only the two most senior members of the Secret Corgi detail were allowed to be a part of the shoot, trailing along right behind Her Majesty the entire time, their eyes constantly on alert for anything untoward. But as it turns out, their eyes weren't the problem."

That comment prompts Victoria to leap in again. "Yes, very much so, indeed. In fact, as far the human guards were concerned, their eyes may have been the sharpest part about them, although being human you really couldn't expect much more of them, I suppose. Anyway, our Ginger, being a mere pup, was relegated to the sidelines the entire time, but since she was so small, especially being the runt of her litter, the other Corgis made an allowance for her to settle down in front of all the adults so she could see what was going on. Otherwise, you understand, her view would have been nothing but Corgi butts and bobbed tails. Astonishingly cute, most certainly, but not much help if you're there to watch closely and learn the proper protocols. And that turned out to be a very good thing, indeed."

Patton One-Eye takes over again, waving one paw for emphasis, and I am glad to see Moose has finally decided to pipe down for a change. All his little "insights" were starting to become quite annoying. Not to mention embarrassing. "You see," One-Eye explains in his overly officious manner, "just as Daniel Craig and the Queen brushed past where Ginger was sitting, it seems the young pup detected something rather off-putting emanating from this Bond fellow. It appears, in fact, that he smelled quite different than he did the day before. Despite her status, Ginger picked up on that difference immediately and took charge. And God bless her little Corgi soul for that."

This story is dragging on so long it's getting increasingly difficult to pay attention. We Corgis just aren't designed for sitting and staring for long periods of time like a bunch of sheep-watching Great Pyrenees, you know. We're dogs bred for constant activity, herders, always on the move. Except, of course, for when we're napping. I glance over at Moose and can see he's starting to drift off, as well. So it's not just me.

I lean over and grab a promising looking biscuit. Food is always a good idea to stir things up when I'm getting bored. Or any time at all, for that matter. "Is this story actually going somewhere?" I ask, trying desperately to speed things along.

One-Eye looks officiously offended. "I must say, I'm surprised you haven't already heard this story. It's quite famous, you know. It was top of the news for several weeks on the PetUK television channel. And made our Ginger into something of a rising star in the canine world."

"No, I'm sorry, we don't get that channel back in America," I explain, crunching down hard on the biscuit. "At least not since my master cut the cord and dropped cable."

Patton nods apologetically. "Oh yes, my mistake, that particular channel is put out by the BBC. Far too sophisticated for colonial tastes, I'm quite sure. Anyway," he continues, apparently not heeding the glowering look I'm now giving him, "as I was saying, Ginger noticed almost immediately that the man walking alongside the Queen smelled nothing at all like the chap who had come to the Palace the day before. I'm not quite sure why the rest of us didn't pick up on that. Star struck, perhaps. It isn't often you get to rub haunches with an actual movie star, you know, and a Bond at that."

"I'm a Double-O agent myself," Moose butts in over his own mouthful of biscuit.

Patton purses his lips, a move that has him looking rather like an overripe cadaver. "Yes, well, that is an interesting little tidbit that we can all discuss at a later date, shall we? But, as I was *saying*—" He throws Moose a scorching glare before continuing. "The Daniel Craig fellow we had seen the day before smelled rather strongly of fine cigars and single malt, apparently his favorite choice of adult beverages when he's not portraying the secret agent at the cinema. But this one, he smelled quite different, indeed. In fact, he absolutely reeked of two rather distinct aromas."

"And what was that?'" I ask impatiently, hoping against hope that we were finally drawing to an end, here.

"Why, it should have been obvious to all of us at first sniff, my dear lady. This man smelled of vodka. A quite pedestrian brand of vodka, at that. And something else. Something even more telling. Beets."

"Yeah? Beets? And why is that important?"

"Why, don't you see? This Bond fellow wasn't a Bond fellow at all. He was no movie star playing a secret agent, he was in fact an honest-to-goodness real secret agent. And a bloody Russian agent, at that!"

Barkingham Palace

I t seems to me that we could have gotten to that little zinger a whole heck of a lot quicker, but I decide to keep that opinion to myself for the time being. I'm still more than a little confused about why we're here, to be perfectly honest, and I'm sure it's not just because of my non-bobbed tail. And then suddenly I realize that I've tuned out once again. And Not-Twin is droning on once more.

"—so Ginger darted out from the pack and latched onto his leg just as tightly as her tiny little milk teeth would allow. We were all quite abashed, as you might imagine, this brash little whelp attacking a guest in the Palace, and Daniel Craig at that! But then he started kicking his legs, trying to fling her off, and without any warning a disturbingly long and colorful string of curse words and other vile invectives exploded from his mouth! And all in Russian, mind you! We picked up on that immediately and rushed forward as a pack to surround the Queen, while the dim-witted human guards eventually came to their senses and grabbed the fellow, his disguise quite literally peeling off his face in one piece, along with his hair. Underneath it all was a beady-eyed sallow-faced Russian agent with nothing more than mere wisps of blondish hair clinging to his pock-marked scalp, fighting off his human captors and snarling and snapping at our Ginger, who had released her death grip on his leg by now and joined the rest of us in protecting Her Majesty. Our little Ginger had saved the day! Saved the Queen from being dognapped and almost certainly tortured by the Russian government!"

"And so now this Ginger person is missing," I remind her, eager to move this along. I take a few laps of water out of the bowl in front of me to wash down the few bits of biscuit that refuse to let go of my tongue, then sit back on my haunches, waiting for a good explanation of what, if any, my role in all this might possibly be.

"Yes, she is," Patton One-Eye says. "And it appears that she's been dognapped herself, but we haven't the foggiest who did it or why."

"Why are you so sure she's been dognapped?" Moose asks. "Maybe someone left one of the back doors open and she's just gone outside for an unsupervised. Happens all the time where I come from."

One-Eye shakes his head impatiently at that. "I assure you, Mr. Moose, she has not gone for an 'unsupervised,' whatever that might be. She is quite firmly committed to her duties here in the Palace. You see, after the incident with the Russian agent, Ginger rose through the ranks quite rapidly to become the lead dog for the Service, reporting only to the UK head of PETSEC. It didn't hurt, of course, that she almost immediately became the Queen's favorite, and as such traveled with Her Majesty almost everywhere she went. A perfect position to watch over the Queen and keep her safe from anyone who might wish to do her harm, don't you see?"

Not-Twin points a paw down at the floor beside her, where a leather-bound notebook is lying. "And we found this just this morning lying on the floor, inside this very room. Ginger's personal diary. Dropped on the carpet, splayed open for anyone and everyone to see. That was not like Ginger at all. There are royal secrets buried in that notebook, things that no one outside of the Royal Family and the Secret Service should ever be privy to."

Moose swings his head slowly around the room. "Okay, but have you checked out all the hiding spots inside the palace? I know sometimes when I have a tummy ache, I like to find someplace private where I can just sleep it off, someplace where nobody is going to bother me."

One-Eye has that offended look on his face again. "That was, of course, the very first thing we addressed. That and interviewing the staff and all of the palace guards. But no one remembered a thing. From the last entries in her diary, we could trace her final steps, of course, the route she took on her usual morning patrol of the Palace, and so we know she was here, in this very room, the last time anyone saw her. Then she just—disappeared. Into thin air, it seems."

"But that doesn't make much sense," I offer. "I mean, I'm not some kind of licensed private detective or secret agent or such, but I'm pretty good at figuring things out, and I know a full-grown Corgi can't just vanish into thin air like that. There has to be some kind of simple explanation to all this, something your people have overlooked."

Victoria Not-Twin evidently took that as a golden opportunity to stare down her long muzzle at me, and her eyes have narrowed down to tiny slits, kind of like mine did when I first saw all the brightly lit gold and chandeliers around here. "I assure you, miss, we have employed only the finest minds in the entire Kingdom for Her Majesty's Secret Service, Corgis and other breeds with the only the most impeccable and unimpeachable training—Oxford, Cambridge, and all that—and they have all come to the very same conclusion. Ginger was dognapped, and somehow spirited out of the Palace under our very noses. In broad daylight, at that."

"So where do we fit into all of this?" Moose asks, breaking the tension that has arisen between me and Queenie V. "And how did you know where to find us?"

One-Eye glances over our heads, waving a paw, and several butlers appear from out of nowhere to whisk away the dog biscuits and water bowls. When they are gone, he clears his throat and continues. "Yes, that. Well I must say, you have made quite a name for yourself in a very short time, Mr. Moose. A very short time indeed. I mean, it's nothing, really, for a dog to pop up out of ignominy to become the hero of the day, that sort of thing happens all the time. It's what we do, after all, we canines. But the usual pattern is, one dog, one act of valor, and that is that. Lassie only saved

Timmy from the well once, you see. So when we heard about this little terrier out in the colonies that managed to save the day for PETSEC and the entire canine race, not once but twice in fact over the span of just one year, well, that had everyone's ears standing at full attention, I can promise you."

"Well, I—" Moose has an embarrassed look plastered across his face, and if it weren't for all the fur it might even have turned bright red. And as usual, those words have me feeling pretty proud for my little Aussie, goofball that he is at times. Pretty much all the time, in fact, if we're being honest.

"I'm kinda surprised those stories made it all the way over here," I say with a shrug. "Much less that anyone paid them any attention."

One-Eye shakes his head, a move that causes his top hat to wobble around precariously on top of his head like a children's top about to fall over on its side. "Notice? Well of course we noticed it! His exploits in fighting off the Russian mob to save PETSEC are famous around the world! Why, without little Moose and his feline friend Tommy Tuxedo, there might not even be an animal world to celebrate such things anymore. Or at least a world that we would recognize."

"So when we heard that he was crossing the pond to join us here in London, we were all positively ecstatic," gushes Victoria Not-Twin. "And, of course, we also heard that he was bringing along a little playmate to keep him company. That would be you, of course."

I know I'm just supposed to be Moose's new big sister and all, and nothing more, but something about that comment makes me go a little green around the edges and red about the ears, if you know what I mean. And that word, the way she said it. Playmate. Seriously? Like I'm supposed to be some kind of toy for him to play with?

Victoria isn't finished gushing, though. "Not that we planned to make a big deal out of it or anything, you understand. We members of the Royal Family are all acutely aware of how much celebrities need their privacy and such, so we just kept tabs on the two of you and bided our time. Then this unfortunate situation popped up all of a sudden, and we immediately thought, what a perfect opportunity to introduce the two of you to the Palace. To Her Majesty's Secret Corgis. Well, officially it's called the Secret Service, but with ninety percent of the detail being Corgis and all…"

"So this is just about doing some kind of informal meet-and-greet? Just a little sniff-the-butt?" I ask, still roundly confused about why we had been summoned all this way across the city at the very last minute with practically zero warning. And in the middle of nappy time, at that.

"Oh no, not at all. Far from it." One-Eye waves a paw in the air in that funny corkscrew fashion of his and a Corgi dressed in a white lab coat appears from out of nowhere carrying a small gray jar of something on a tiny silver platter. And when I say white lab coat, what I mean is a laboratory coat, not the fur off an actual white Lab. That would be unspeakably cruel.

Not-Twin is droning on again. "—so you see, Ginger has become a constant presence in the Palace now, and with her distinctive coloration and un-docked tail, her absence among the Corgis will almost certainly be noted rather quickly by the humans around here. That's why we needed a stand-in, a Corgi who can play the part of Ginger until we can rescue her and bring her back to the Palace."

Okay, now I'm starting to understand what this is all about. Not-Twin wants me to play the part of a real twin. And I get the fact that humans are all so stupid they have problems telling us Corgis apart. But there's just one little worm still wiggling around inside her whole half-baked plan.

"Well, that's a brilliant idea and all that," I say, trying but not entirely succeeding in keeping the sarcasm out of my voice. "But really, don't you think even a dumb human will notice that I'm not a red-head?"

Not-Twin smiles at me like I've said something totally idiotic. And she doesn't bother with trying to hide her own sarcasm for even a second. "Oh that little thing. Posh, that's not a bother at all." She nods in the direction of Lab Coat, who immediately screws the lid off the small jar he's holding. "Q'ute Branch has developed a henna-based red dye that will do the trick of turning you into a Ginger quite nicely. It will only take a minute or so to apply, and in the end you'll be for all intents and purposes the spitting image of our Ginger. Or at least, close enough that the humans will never be able to tell the difference." She glances down at her paws for a moment before returning her gaze to

47

me. "Well, most humans, that is. And of course, any resemblance will only be skin deep, you understand. There is only one true Ginger, after all, and I have very little doubt that Her Majesty will see through our little ruse almost immediately. And that's why it is absolutely imperative that we locate the real Ginger on the double."

"W-e-l-l, okay, I suppose." I take a quick sniff of whatever is in the little jar, and it doesn't give off much of an odor at all. Which you might find a bit strange, my caring about that, seeing as how I love to roll around in dead stuff, but there's a huge difference between the natural scent of nicely rotting flesh and something all chemical-like, don't you agree? "But how long will this red stuff last? And will it rub off easily? I can't be jumping up on my mistress' couch if I'm going to mess everything up, you know. Leave behind any tell-tale stains." That wouldn't do at all.

"Don't worry, it won't rub off, and it won't come off with soap and water. The lab rats assure me it can only be removed with another special cream, one that will return your coat to its original if unremarkable color."

"Very well, then," I tell her with a sigh. "Let's get it over with, I suppose."

While they're busy rubbing the reddening cream on me, General One-Eye gives Moose a light cuffing on the shoulder. "And with that little detail out of the way, it's well past time for us to get our own backsides in gear and take charge of the search for our fearless leader. Moose, I'm going to be busy coordinating everything from PETSEC headquarters back in the Tower, but we desperately need a trained and experienced agent like yourself out in the field. That is, if you don't mind lending a paw to the effort."

Moose looks confused, which admittedly is not all that uncommon for him. "Field? You think Ginger's being held on a farm somewhere? But I suppose that would make good sense, given how loud Corgis are and all. You just can't get them to shut up most days. If she was in the city, she'd be located right away, for sure. There would be no real way to keep her quiet."

Patton shakes his head at that, now looking somewhat confused himself. "No, Moose, not that kind of field agent." He looks my way for support, and all I can do is shrug my shoulders. "Anyway, you'll be working with one of our top agents. Dodger is his name, a Norwich Terrier with the most impeccable credentials. Ah, and here he is now."

Trotting across the carpet toward us is a small, straw-colored dog, about the size of Moose with short legs, up-turned ears and a long fox-like face. He gives us a big grin and a waggle of his stubby tail.

"Why 'ello there, Ginger, General, Victoria. An' who might we 'ave 'ere?"

General One-Eye takes a step forward to make the introductions. "Dodger, this is Moose, Moose McGillicutty. From off across the pond."

Dodger steps back a pace and eyes Moose over from ear to tail. "O-o-h," he says, drawing the word out over several syllables. "I must say, I rather expected the famous American agent to be a might—larger, given all 'is exploits. But 'ey, fight in the dog an' all that, as they say. Good to make yer acquaintance, Mr. Moose."

He shoves out a paw and Moose leans forward to shake it. "Likewise, Dodger. But tell me, what kind of dog is a Norwich Terrier, by the way? I can't say I've ever met one before. And I've met a lot of dogs in my day. Particularly after we broke all of the dogs out of the prison and all. But never a Norwich, at least as far as I can recall."

"Oh, we're quite common where I come from, that's for sure. But we're often mistaken for Norfolk Terriers, which has never made sense to me, being that we're nothing at all alike. It's all in the ears, you see. Ours are far superior."

I am quite certain Moose has no idea what this Dodger fellow is talking about, as I don't either, when Victoria speaks up again, that grating voice of hers rasping off the walls in the room like fingernails on a sidewalk.

"Oh, and Dodger, I'm afraid you've mistaken our friend Bella here for our own dear Ginger. Bella is an old companion of Moose's, currently staying with him on a yacht out at Limehouse Marina. In the East End."

"Gor blimey love a duck!" Dodger gives me the once-over, just as he did Moose a bit earlier. "Can't say I can tell the difference, she even 'as the non-bobbed tail. And the red 'air. Are you from Bath, as well?"

Dodger's use of the name "Bath" leaves me with an involuntary shiver. Shaking off the image of a bathie, I look down at my paws, then back at my tail.

51

They really did do a good job with the cream, it all looks perfectly natural. "No, we're from Chicago, actually," I tell him. "Moose and I. Our master got a new posting here in London, so we moved here about a month ago. Actually, this is our very first trip into London proper. Although we were in such a hurry getting here this morning, I can't say I've seen much of your city yet. It was all pretty much a blur."

One-Eye is checking his watch. "Yes, it's all sixes and sevens around here this morning, I'm afraid. You see, Dodger, and please keep this under your collar, but it seems our Ginger has been dognapped."

"Dognapped, you say! Ginger?"

"Yes, and that's why we've called you here. Bella has agreed to act as a stand-in for her here at the Palace, to keep the humans from getting in a kerfluffle about her disappearance, while Victoria has ordered an all-dogs-on-deck search throughout the city for our leader. I can only hope we find her in time before—"

The room suddenly goes completely quiet as all of us consider the implications of what was just not said. That Ginger might not have been dognapped at all. That she may have been—murdered—instead.

One-Eye finally breaks the awkwardness, staring at his watch again.

"Well, what are we all doing standing around in our jim jams gabbing like we've got nothing else to do? Moose, you go with Dodger, here, he'll serve as your assistant, help you out any way he can. I'm off to the Tower of London to oversee the search efforts. Victoria, while Bella here is more than adequate to keep the humans at bay in the Palace, we still need someone on station to protect the Royals and make sure we've turned over every possible leaf within these walls, every possible clue Ginger might have left behind to lead us to her." He stops talking long enough to give Moose a long hard stare with that disconcerting eye of his. "And Moose, we're all counting on you to come through for us in this one. If ever we needed someone to pull a right blinder—" He glanced in Dodger's direction. "You know, pull off some kind of miracle, it's now. We've got no leads, no idea where Ginger might be, or how they even got her out of Barkingham Palace in the first place, given the guards and cameras we have watching every single exit. But somehow they did it, and now we are quickly running out of time to hunt her down. And I don't need to tell you, time is a luxury Ginger may be quite lacking at the moment. So Moose—don't let us down, laddie. Find her. And find her fast."

Moose

Barkingham Palace

S o what's our first move, guv?" Dodger asks as we head in the direction of no destination in particular.

I shake my head, completely befuddled by everything that's happened since Patton whats-his-name so rudely jarred me awake this morning. "I—I don't know. I sorta thought you might have some ideas. You know, since this is kind of your home turf and all."

"Oh, sure. Well, we could start by checkin' in with Q'ute, I suppose. She usually 'as her nose to the wind on these kind of things."

"Q'ute? You mean she's here in London? Whoa ho! The old girl certainly gets around, doesn't she?"

"Here? In London? Old? You sure we're talkin' about the same dog?" Dodger points me toward a small alcove just off the hallway, at the end of which is some kind of tall red metal box with glass windows on every side. He races up to the box and pulls open a door, a move that takes quite a bit of effort by the looks of things. "Wait 'ere, mate. I'll be just a second," he says before jumping inside, the door slamming shut right behind him.

Once inside the box he hops up on a small metal stool, then starts poking around some kind of a keyboard mounted on the front of a smaller, odd-looking metal box hanging on a side wall. After a few seconds he hops back out and closes the door.

"It'll be just a moment. They'll probably 'ave to knock her up, given the time difference between here and Chicago."

Almost a minute passes and I'm about ready to give up on whatever Dodger has planned, when all of a sudden the lights in the alcove start to dim and a strange smoky blue light comes on inside the metal box. The blue light pulses, then begins to take shape, and in mere moments I'm looking straight on at a ghostly version of my old friend Q'ute!

"You didn't tell me she died!" I tell Dodger, grabbing him by the shoulders, my alarm readily apparent in the suddenly shrill sound of my voice. Kind of like the sound a Chihuahua makes when it sees its master.

Dodger shakes me off. "No, it's not that, Mr. Moose, really it's not. It's just an 'ologram is all. A 3D kind of telly. It's all the rage these days, innit?"

Q'ute's ghost has started talking, and I settle down and shush Dodger so I can hear what she's saying. I've never talked to a dead person before, and I don't want to miss this chance. It may very well be my last.

"—good to see you again, Moose. But really, what in the world is going on that justifies a call like this in the middle of the night?"

Q'ute had obviously been dead asleep, and she's standing there now in her jammies, wearing a simple robe and cute little bunny slippers so lifelike I almost want to jump inside the metal box and bite them.

"Our deepest apologies," Dodger is saying to the Q'ute-in-the-box. "Things have gone a bit barmy over here, and we need your 'elp quite desperately. It seems Ginger has suddenly gone missing."

"Missing? Ginger? Well, that is a bit bonkers, for sure. She is, if anything, absolutely the most reliable dog I have ever met, so this must be serious. When exactly did this happen?"

"Sometime this mornin', ma'am. She was out on rounds, and then poof!, she was gone. They've searched the Palace from the rafters to the knickers but we've 'ad no luck, no luck at all. So we turned to you, of course, to see if anything 'as popped up on all those sneaky little ears you 'ave 'idden about the city."

"Oh! Of course! One moment, please." Q'ute disappears from the metal box for a moment before suddenly reappearing. It all looks like black magic to me. And, knowing Q'ute, it probably mostly is.

"Okay, I don't have anything directly on point, but we did get word that our old friend Vladimir Kitn has been seen in and about the London area over the past few weeks. We have no idea what he's up to, but knowing Kitn it can't be good."

"Kitn!" I blurt out. I had really hoped I'd seen the last of that mangy Russian cat. But clearly those hopes have now been dashed. Not the first time that's happened, unfortunately. And it probably won't be the last. I lean in a little closer, my thoughts coming in a rush. "Are you sure? Given what he tried to pull in Chicago with disrupting the PETSEC elections, I wouldn't put it past him to be right in the middle of all this. But why? How could it possibly help him to dognap a Corgi? And a highly recognizable Corgi at that?"

Q'ute is nodding. "I'm with you on that, Moose. But yes, one of our agents trailed Kitn to Victoria Station, where he managed to slip their collar somehow. From Victoria you can easily get transport to anywhere else in the city. Or the world, for that matter. So it may be just a wild goose chase, but at least it's a reasonable place to start." She eases toward me a little, squinting. "And Moose, I see you've still got that blue collar we gave you when you were working back here in the city with Tommy Tuxedo."

"Yeah, I half expected one of my humans to notice it and replace it with a regular collar, but they haven't exactly been in a talkative mood with each other lately, and I guess they each must have thought the other bought it to replace my old leather collar." And not that I would have said anything. My old collar was getting a bit ratty, I'll have to admit. And all those trips digging under the fence behind the old mulberry bush didn't exactly help.

Q'ute is smiling at me, and for some reason it's making my tummy feel a little queasy all of a sudden, like it does when I've wolfed down an old chewstick

I've found buried out in the yard, except in a nice sorta way. "Well, that's wonderful news! It means I won't have to send you over to the lab to get another one, which saves us a great deal of time. Not to mention money, since those collars don't exactly come cheap. Do you still remember how the collar phone works?"

"Collar phone? You mean the whole tap-tap thing? Kinda sorta. I never really ever used it myself, and to tell the truth I didn't know my collar even worked that way, but I saw Tommy make and receive calls with his several times. You just kinda hit the side of it with your paw, and then say whoever it is you need to talk to, and the collar does the rest. Is that about right?"

"Yes, Moose, that is exactly right. The collar is actually sending and receiving constantly whenever we have it activated, which I will take care to make happen right away. We'll have operators monitoring it nonstop, tracking your movements and patching calls through for you. And, hold on…" She appears to be staring at something off-box. "Good, you still have well over 80 percent power left, which should hold you for several more days, even with heavy use. You two head on over to Victoria, then, and start poking around.

I'll give you a call just as soon as I find anything out." She pauses, like she has just remembered something critical. "Oh, and Moose, that collar has a few other neat tricks hidden away inside that may wind up being pretty useful over the next few days. When we have a little more time, I'll walk you through it all. But the most important thing to remember right now is, if you find yourself in a scrape and something or someone tries to bite your head off at the neck, go ahead and let them."

"What? You've got to be kidding me! Why in the world would I let someone—"

"You've just got to trust me on this one, Moose. Let's just say if they bite down on your neck they're going to get a very bad taste in their mouth. A very bad taste indeed." She glances down at the watch on her wrist. "But we can talk about all that later. You two need to make double time for Victoria Station, and I need to get to my office and start digging into whatever Kitn has up his sleeve right about now. It's high time that pestilent pussy came to face his own personal Waterloo, don't you know. His final, humiliating battle, that is, not the Tube station."

I almost giggle, remembering that Vladimir Kitn doesn't actually have a sleeve. Or much in the way of fur at all for that matter. And I didn't get that last point at all. Waterloo. Isn't that what the English call a toilet?

But she's right, time's a-wasting. I grab Dodger by the shoulder and point him toward the Mews gift shop, our exit out of the palace. It's well past time for Double-O-Ten to get to work.

Victoria Station

The station is hopping with activity like a back yard bunny convention, with trains coming and going pretty much non-stop. Crowds of locals and tourists are streaming back and forth between the trains, the Tube station and the various assorted forms of above-ground transportation, all of the humans pretty much doing everything they can to ignore everyone around them. I pass by a tourist shop selling a bunch of Paddington Bear merchandise, and looking in I can suddenly fully understand his sense of total bewilderment upon first stepping foot in all this chaos. As for myself, I have absolutely no inkling of where to start looking for our mortal enemy, Vladimir Kitn. And that's right when my collar decides to start buzzing like a swarm of mad bees.

Dodger is pointing at something on the far side of the station and tugging hard on my arm, even as I'm slapping at my neck, trying to get the collar to calm down. People are starting to turn and look at me, so I decide to try another tack. "Uh, Hey Google? Alexa? Siri? Anybody there?"

That seems to have worked, somehow, because my collar has stopped buzzing, but now I've got Dodger looking at me strangely as well. "Look, Moose," he says after a long moment, his head cocked slightly to one side as he stares at me like I've lost my mind. "There's a tourist booth over near the exits. That's where our command center for the station is located. We should start there."

"A command center?" I have to ask. "Here? In a train station? Isn't that kinda overkill?" I mean, Chicago is PETSEC world headquarters, but even at the HQ we never bothered to cover any of the "L" stations.

Dodger answers me, looking off again toward the other side of the station. "Victoria Station is one of the primary transportation 'ubs for the entire city of London, and in some ways for the entire country. If anything is 'appening in England, at some point it will probably 'ave to travel through 'ere."

"And this is where they first located Kitn. Okay, it all makes sense now. Let's go."

Just as we start off, though, my collar buzzes again, but this time I remember the trick about lightly tapping it on the right side. "Agent Double-O-Ten here," I woof quietly out of the right side of my mouth.

"Double-O-Ten?" The voice sounds loudly in my ears, clear enough to me even though somehow nobody else seems to hear it, Dodger included. "I'm sorry, I'm trying to reach Moose McGillicutty. I must have the wrong—"

"No, no, this is Moose." This must be one of those operators Q'ute said she'd have standing by, but obviously he hadn't gotten the memo yet about my secret agent status. Maybe it got stuck in a personnel file or something back in Chicago. I'll just have to follow up on that later, I suppose. But, meanwhile, back to the call. "You got something for me?"

"Uh, yes, we just wanted to confirm that your collar is now fully activated, and wondered if you have any questions about your service. It says here we have you on the unlimited data plan, which is our top of the line option, and if you would like we can add an additional collar to your account for no extra charge. Other than the cost for the collar, of course, which we can space out over twenty-four low monthly payments at the introductory price of only—"

What the—is this guy for real? Spaced out is right on the money for this fellow. "Look, uh, I'm kind of busy at the moment saving the free world," I tell him, cutting him off mid-stream. "Could you call back later?"

"Uh, sure, no problem. What time—"

I tap the side of my collar again to cut him off completely, then signal to Dodger—who's staring at me strangely again—that it's well past time to move on ahead.

Getting through the crowd in the station is no small feat, mostly because the crowd is pretty much all feet, and none of them are in fact all that small, but eventually we pull up in front of the tourist booth, a small shop selling maps and tickets and cheap Chinese-made English souvenirs. Dodger leads us inside, ducking under a swinging wooden door keeping the tourists at bay on the right side of the counter, and then he slips through a side door to the back of the shop. Once again, the humans running the store seem to be making a great effort not to notice us. Unlike how they'd be back home in Chicago, for sure, where they'd almost certainly be trying to toss us back outside, or capture us to turn us over to the concentration camp guards. Must have something to do with how the English all seem to love their pets.

I'm still working through all this in my head and basically following Dodger on autopilot when suddenly my auto cruise control fails me and I crash into his backside, sending both of us scattering like bowling pins.

"Oof! Watch it mate!" Dodger complains as he pulls himself back to his feet.

"Sorry," is all I have to say for myself, and I try to cover my mistake by stopping to take a good long look around. We're in a small back room of the store, and every single wall in the room has a tall stack of flat-screen monitors showing almost every single corner and crevice in the station. Beneath each bank of monitors is a control desk lined with buttons and switches, each of the desks under the careful command of a breed of dog I don't immediately recognize. Mid-size, sorta, with medium-long black and white fur and floppy ears. They're all busy pushing buttons and pulling levers, and every time they do so the images flicker and change above their heads.

"Morning, Dodger," one of them says without bothering to turn around. "Who's the bloke?"

69

"How—" I start to sputter as Dodger simply smiles back at me.

"They 'ad a bead on us the moment we stepped paw in the station," Dodger explains, pointing a paw toward a monitor that was at that very moment showing a recording of our entrance just a few minutes earlier. He turns his attention back to the speaker. "This 'ere's none other than Moose, Moose McGillicutty. In the flesh."

This time the dog turns around completely and scopes me out slowly from top to bottom. A live picture of me pops up on a monitor on each of the other three walls at the same time. "Well I'll be buggered," he says. "Never thought for the life of me I'd ever have the honor. Nice to make your acquaintance, Agent Moose." The other three dogs woof their agreement, as well, all four of their tails wagging furiously. "What brings you all the way out to our neck of the woods, might I ask? Mind you, I'm not complaining."

Dodger grabs a cushion from one corner of the room and sits down, motioning for me to do the same. "We're 'ere because of your reported sighting of Vladimir Kitn. We thought you might be able to shed some light on where he might 'ave disappeared off to."

"Disappeared is an apt phrase for it," said one of the other dogs, who was already back at work at his desk, punching buttons. "Here, you can see what we got. We had the cameras tracking him all the way through the station. But then, Crikey Moses, he was gone with not so much as a poof! Now you see him, now you don't. Like a regular Houdini, he was."

He pulls on a lever and a video starts playing on a screen above his head. It was Kitn, all right, just like I'd seen him back in Chicago several months before. Same patchy fur, same cocky walk—which I suppose he picked up somehow to try and compensate for how amazingly ugly he is. The cameras were doing an amazing job of keeping track of him moving across the station, following almost the same exact path we did, when all of a sudden he stops, standing all by himself in the very middle of the station, staring straight up at the camera swiping at his whiskers with one paw, and then simply vanishes without a trace. Just like he did outside of Macy's in Chicago, with Tommy Tuxedo and I standing right in front of him, not twenty feet away.

Dodger is rubbing his eyes with his own paw like somehow that's going to make Kitn magically reappear, but I know that's not going to happen.

"When exactly was this video taken?" I ask the first dog, breaking the tension in the room.

"Yesterday morning," another dog answers. "Check the time stamp in the corner."

How stupid of me. Of course, there it was, plain as the nose on my face. Once again, even after all these other dogs were falling all over each other to praise my vaunted talents as a secret agent, I know the honest truth of the matter—so far my only real talent in the secret agent business has been plain dumb luck. With an emphasis on the dumb part. But that doesn't mean I need to stop trying, stop doing my part to try and locate Ginger. After all, even a blind dog finds a bone every once in a while. I give my head a quick shake to clear my thoughts and turn back to face Dodger.

"I've seen this little magic trick before, a few months ago back in Chicago. Kitn had escaped a human dragnet Tommy Tuxedo and I dropped on him and his greasy minions, and apparently he decided to use that as a good opportunity to rub it in. But the question we're facing here is, why? Why make his presence here so obvious to everyone involved? And what exactly is he up to here in London? This couldn't have been just a random accident of some kind. That's not Kitn's style."

"No, yer right about that," Dodger says, looking back at the video that is still running on the monitor above our heads, absent one particularly hideous feline. "An' for certain there's no way it isn't connected somehow to Ginger's disappearance. But the question for us now is, what 'ole 'as he dropped off into?" Dodger turns his eyes toward the first dog we'd spoken to. "Are you sure there isn't any other evidence of 'is whereabouts? No other camera in the city caught 'im, even for a moment?"

"No, we ran muzzle recognition software on every feed we have, and you know, ever since that terrorist bombing back in 2005 we pretty much have an eye on every square inch of the city. But so far, nothing has turned up, nothing at all. But, hey, what's that you said about Ginger? She's up and disappeared? When did that happen?"

Dodger slaps the side of his head with one paw. Hard. We'd been specifically instructed to keep the Ginger situation under our fur, and now he'd gone and spilled the kibble to the very first dog he'd talked to. Well, actually, four dogs, come to think of it. But there's nothing we can do about it at this point except come clean, I figure. And see if we can enlist their help in trying to find her.

I carefully lay out everything we know about her dognapping, which isn't much. "So you see, it only makes sense that Kitn is involved, somehow. That's why we decided to start here, to see if we could catch a warm lead onto his trail."

"Well, I'm afraid that after a full day with thousands of humans stomping through Victoria Station, that trail's gone ice cold," Watch Dog Number One says. "But we can rerun the muzzle recognition software to see if we can spot Ginger. After all, there can't be all that many red-haired long-tailed Corgis running around in this city, even as big and busy as it is. I'll get jumping on that right away."

"Thanks," Dodger says, looking grateful that I've managed to turn his little gaffe around for us, managed to turn it into some kind of a net positive for the investigation. "But, by the way, keep the news about Ginger on the downlow, if you don't mind. It's all gone a bit Pete Tong today around the Palace."

"No. Absolutely." Watch Dog gives us the paws-up sign as the other three dogs nod away in vigorous agreement. "But say we manage to turn up something, how do we get in touch with you?"

"Moose 'as a blue collar," Dodger explains without any further comment, leaving me to wonder just how many dogs knew about the secret tech I've been wearing right out in the open, plain as day for several months now, not even imagining it had any greater power or utility than to simply unlock my electronic doggie door.

"Gotcha. Okay, we'll just relay anything we find through Q'ute Branch. We'll get right on it."

"Smashing," Dodger tells him as we turn to make our escape, leaving me wondering how in the world breaking something could ever help our investigation. But hey, as it turns out I've apparently been wearing some kind of a magical blue collar for the past few months and been none the wiser for it, so in this crazy new land I now find myself in, I guess you just never know…

Embankment

For the life of me I have no earthly idea why I've let Dodger talk me into this exceedingly dodgy adventure. Traveling by boat, of all things! It's only been a few months since the last time I set paw on a boat—well, a boat that moves, at least—and I swore back then it would be my last.

We're standing on a dock looking out over the Thames, and a line of ferry boats is moored up alongside, ready to take on any tourists and a good smattering of the locals down the river to Greenwich, which apparently is somehow worth the time and expense to see. But as for me, I wouldn't care if it was a Sandwich, I'm sure as shooting not jumping on any boats!

I prod Dodger, who's standing close beside me. "Tell me again why this is such a good idea?"

He's been busy poring over a schedule of some sorts, and he looks up, somewhat startled. "Good idea? Well, I can't rightly say it is all that, guv, but given that we've got no other leads at present as to Ginger's likely whereabouts, I'd 'ave to say it's the only prospect that makes any sense. We take the ferry down the river and 'op off at the Tower of London, like I said. At this time of day, with all the crowds pressing into the Tube, it would take us three times as long to make the journey using the Underground, even assuming we weren't crushed underfoot in the process like so much unseen rubbish."

I'm still not completely sold on the idea, and I let him know. "Okay, I get that much, but why the Tower of London? Isn't that just some kind of pricey tourist trap? I can't see how taking in the sights of London can help us in any way at this point."

Dodger gives me a sour look, like his human mistress has just brought home a litter of kittens. "Tourist trap? I assure you, Mr. Moose, the Tower is far more than that. Why, much of the storied 'istory of London—and all of jolly old England, for that matter—is largely boxed up within those walls, even if it 'as gotten a might posh these days. But no, we're not going *up* in the Tower, we're going down. PETSEC's UK headquarters is located in the dungeons far beneath the old girl, and if we're going to gen up on what's afoot with Vladimir Kitn and his like, that's the best place to start."

Okay, that makes sense. I suppose. "So you're saying we can take a ferry down the river, and it will pull up next to the Tower to let the tourists off, and we can jump off with them?"

"Oh, no, but that would all be easy peasy if it worked out that way, right? The problem with that approach, though, is that the entrance to PETSEC HQ is top secret, so it 'as to be accessed in a way that keeps all the tourists safely at bay."

Now that he says that, I can remember the secret entrance to Q'ute's laboratory in Chicago, plummeting into a lightless hole in the sidewalk and dropping several stories before crashing into a safety net at the bottom. I certainly don't want to relive that particular experience again. In contrast, a boat ride doesn't seem all that bad all of a sudden.

"Okay, Dodger, so if the ferry doesn't dock at the Tower, how in the world do we get from here to there. And please don't tell me we have to swim." If I knew I'd be in for a bathies, I think I might have reconsidered the whole thing, Ginger or no.

Dodgers grins at me. "I'm with you on that, Moose. But no, I've got somethin' else in mind. This isn't the first time someone's taken the ferry to the Tower, believe me."

He doesn't go into any more details, so I decide to just bite my tongue for the time being. After all, it's not like I have a long list of alternative ideas at the moment. After studying the schedule again, Dodger seems to make up his mind and points out a ferry toward the end of the dock.

"There. That one. Get ready to move, they're just about to throw off the ropes. That'll be our signal to jump on board at the last moment."

Sure enough, as we waddle as inconspicuously as we can toward the boat, a man dressed in some kind of official-looking uniform hops down off the front and begins to untie the lines holding the ferry tight to the side of the shore. When he's done, he moves to the rear of the boat and begins to undo that set of ropes as well. He turns his back to us for just a second, then Dodger gives me the high sign and we dash forward, leaving our cover behind as we leap across the short gap from the dock to the boat entrance and land hard on the other side.

"Oof!" I say, and Dodger looks my way and shushes me, then races lickety-split toward a small pile of ropes that have been coiled up near the back. And the timing couldn't have been any better—no sooner are we tucked in safely in our little hidey-hole than the boat lurches forward and starts off on its journey down the river.

The rope guy walks past us without even once glancing our way, and when he's gone I turn back to Dodger. "Okay, we made it onto the boat by the skin of our eye teeth. What's next?"

Dodger checks over his shoulder to make sure nobody's noticed us, then turns back and points at my collar. "Yeah, this is where we need to call ahead and let them know we're comin'. As you might imagine, it's generally a bad idea to knock them up without prior notice. That's a good way of turning everythin' into a bit of a dog's dinner, you know? Last bloke who tried that was last seen floatin' down the Thames toward the open sea. Ruined his whole day, the little duffer." He pauses and gives me a wide smile. "But not to bother, guv. Just tap that little collar of yours and I'll 'andle all the details."

His explanation has left me at a bit at bit of a loss, but I do as he says, reaching up to tap the right side of my collar. Almost instantly a Limey voice rings out in my ears.

"Yes, Mr. Moose? How can I be of most excellent service to you today?"

Dodger leans in and speaks to the left side of my collar, keeping his voice low but precise to avoid drawing any unnecessary attention to us. "Yes, HQ, this is Dodger. Put it on speaker, please."

The collar crackles slightly, and now the voice coming from it is slightly louder, and from Dodger's expression I can see that he can hear the voice coming from the collar, as well. "Yes, Dodger, what do you need?"

Dodger pulls back just a bit and drops his voice a notch lower. Evidently, speaker mode can easily handle this quieter exchange. "Moose and I are on the Thames Clipper that just left Embankment bound for Greenwich. We need you to make arrangements for us to disembark at the Tower so we can pay a visit to HQ."

"Certainly. I have the ferry schedule up on my screen right now. We have you coming alongside in about fifteen minutes. I'll make all the arrangements for a transfer. I take it both of you are coming over?"

Dodger nods, even though the move clearly can't be seen over the sound-only collar contraption. Or at least I think it's sound only. "Yes. Both Moose and I will be transferrin'."

"Very well. Stand by. I'll ring up Moose when we're ready for you."

I can hear the collar click and suddenly the line goes dead. I look over at Dodger with a questioning expression.

"Okay, Moose, now we sit and wait." He pulls out a dog biscuit from someplace I can't see. "As they say, bite'em if you got'em," he says and chomps down with obvious relish. After a few seconds of chewing, he suddenly seems to notice the look on my face. "Oh, sorry! Where are my manners?"

He reaches up into his collar and pulls out another biscuit, handing it over rather sheepishly.

"Thanks," I say, grabbing the small bite-size biscuit and tying into it immediately, wagging my thanks the entire time. I wish I could say I sat back and relished it, but that really isn't my nature. In my heart, I'm way more a wolf than I am a purse doggie, and in just a matter of seconds I'm busily licking my paws and wishing I had taken a little more time with it.

Dodger is equally wolf-like, and settles back as well, both of us watching and waiting as the shoreline of London slides by before us. The sun is shining on my fur, and I've just drifted off to a well-deserved sleep when suddenly I'm rudely shaken awake by a loud buzzing coming from my collar. Rubbing a paw across my eyes to wake up, I finally reach up and tap the side, and the voice comes alive through the back of my ears again.

"Clear to put it on speaker?" the voice asks with a slight growl.

"Sure," I say, and once again the collar crackles and the voice lowers to a near whisper.

"Agents Moose and Dodger, we'll have a launch coming alongside in sixty seconds. Be ready."

"Rodger," says Dodger, and points with one paw toward the looming battlements of the Tower of London coming up on our left, then the general location on the side of the boat where we first came on board. "They'll be pullin' up there," he says, wagging his paw for emphasis. "Be ready to move out on my signal."

I wag my tail back at him, then glance around to see if we're being watched. The rope handler is standing not ten feet away, and it's hard to believe that he hasn't seen us at this point since we're both sitting pretty much in broad daylight despite all the ropes, but like all the other humans we've come across in the little shops on land he seems adamant about looking pretty much in any direction but ours. Odd.

I'm not very good about telling time, other than having a dead-on sense of exactly when my meals are supposed to be served, but it seems like no time before Dodger pulls up one paw and brings it down sharply, then leaps up and sprints at full speed toward the Tower side of the boat, with me right behind him. There's a short wall around most of the rear of the boat, but it's missing right in front of us, and instead there's a fat yellow rope stretched across the gap, well above our heads. I can't see anything else in front of us but water, and I'm just about to pull up short when suddenly Dodger gives it an extra burst of speed and leaps out into the open air! I'm so surprised by that crazy move that I miss my last slippery opportunity to slide to a stop, and before I know it I'm right at the edge, leaping out into the void right behind him. I guess now is when I finally find out whether dogs are born knowing how to dogpaddle, or whether we have to be taught, because if it's the latter, I'm sure as shooting going to be walking to the Tower by way of the bottom of the river! Or, more likely, floating down it out to sea like that poor fellow Dodger told me about.

The Thames

I hit hard, landing on my left side, and even though I've pressed my lips together tight as a tick to hold in my final few breaths, all that air gets squished out of my lungs on impact. I brace myself for the chill of the frigid river water, but that doesn't happen, and when I finally squeeze my eyes open, I find I'm lying somewhere high and dry! Or, to be more accurate, low and dry. Rolling over on my back, I can see Dodger standing right beside me on all fours, staring down at me with a look of real concern smeared across his face.

"I say, Mr. Moose, are you all right?" he asks, reaching a paw down to help me up. "You look like you've just been kicked in the goolies."

"Uh, yeah, I guess so." I finally get all my paws under me and stand up myself, my left side screaming at me the whole while. "I, uh, I think I may have messed up my ribs or something when I landed, though." I look around, and everything about me is all a featureless dark gray, just like the river. But we're apparently standing on dry ground, somehow, so it can't be—

86

Dodger's look goes from concerned to embarrassed in a flash. "Oh, right! Sorry, guv'nor, my bad! I should have warned you about the boat."

As soon as he said it I got it. Before we jumped off the ferry, a small gray rubber dinghy had pulled up alongside to retrieve us and take us to the Tower. It all makes perfect sense now. If I'd been taller, like a human, I would have noticed it right away.

I decide the best move to make here is to cover my own embarrassment at not being wise to the now quite obvious master plan. "No, I was onto it the whole time," I lie, with what I hope is a straight face. "Just must have slipped on a puddle of water when I jumped. They really should watch that, you know. Someone could get hurt."

One thing I do happen to notice right away is that there's no driver. As far as I can tell, Dodger and I are the only people on board the little rubber dinghy. "Hey, by the way, who the heck's steering this darn thing?" I ask, checking all around the back of the boat for some sign of a tiller or steering wheel.

"No need for that," Dodger answers with a grin. "Everything's robotic these days. M likes it that way. She says the fewer eyes on what's going on down below the Tower, the less we 'ave to worry about leaks. Like the one you dug up at Q'ute's labs in Chicago. She's even got a sign on her desk, 'For My Eyes Only' it says. Pretty much says it all."

Dodger turns to face the shoreline beside the tower, which is coming up on us pretty quickly. We seem to be aiming toward a gate of some sort that is ever so slowly rising up out of the water, creaking noisily the entire time. The gate is made of thick overlapping bands of black iron, kind of like the top of the fruit pies Helen makes every now and then, except of course they're iron, and as the bottom of the gate emerges from the gray water I can see that it has sharp spikes lined up in a neat row along the bottom.

We pull up close, and before we can slip underneath the gate it stops suddenly, forcing Dodger and I to duck down at the last minute to keep from getting debrained by the spikes as we slide under.

"You think they'd fix that!" Dodger complains, using a loud voice to carry over the roar of the dinghy's motor and the sound of the gate drawing closed behind us. "Just last week a bloke got 'imself a right nasty 'aircut, he did! Took twenty bloody stitches to fix 'im up. And I mean bloody in the most literal sense."

I shake my head sharply to try and clear that image out of my mind. I'm every bit as brave as the next fellow, but I can't say I'm all that good about the whole blood thing. Unless of course it comes connected to a nice slice of meat or a juicy bone. That goes without saying, you know. Although I guess I did just say it.

Dodger is climbing up over the side of the dinghy onto dry land, and I follow him without a single word passing between us. That's just basic spycraft, after all, keeping the verbal communications to a minimum in case anyone's listening in.

Once I've made it over the side I find myself on a wide but narrow stretch of concrete. Or maybe it's just rock—in the dim light it's hard to be sure which—and there's a solid-looking metal door off to our right that's sunk into the wall like it's never letting go. I give Dodger a meaningful look, then glance back at the door, then back again to Dodger, and he nods knowingly.

"Unless you plan on diggin' to Chiner, that's the way in, Moosey." He walks over to a pewter panel set into the stone wall to the right of the door and seems to be tapping out some kind of code, but after several fruitless tries he steps back, frowning. Finally he turns toward me and growls, the kind of growl you give when you've got a bone and other dogs are starting to trespass into your personal space, and then he glances up at my collar, does a weird kind of shoulder roll, and calls out in a really loud voice "Collar, open tower door."

Immediately the door responds, sliding open with the kind of gut-wrenching grating noise you really only expect from something maybe 100 or so dog years old, really ancient, and suddenly we're looking at—

An elevator. Well, at least I think it's an elevator. It's a box set in a wall with only one way in or out, so unless the plan is to put us into solitary confinement for some reason, it would have to be an elevator. Besides, you can't put two guys into solitary together, that just doesn't work. That's why they call it solitary, after all.

Anyway, we quickly jump inside, Dodger presses the down button and I can feel the whole floor-dropping-out-from-under-me sensation that tells me we're on our way. And judging by the feel of things, we're moving fast.

I suddenly realize I've been following Dodger's lead on all this ever since we left Barkingham Palace, and this might be a good time to catch up with the master plan he evidently has cooked up in that tiny terrier brain of his. Not that there's anything wrong with tiny terrier brains. Just saying.

"So, where's this thing taking us?" I ask, trying to sound all casual about it.

"This is a direct elevator to M's office," he answers, all the while watching a small display over our heads that's ticking through numbers one after one, like a countdown or something. "Her office is at the very bottom of the facility, bomb proof and all that, you know."

"Right." I wave one paw around in the air. "So all this, is this PETSEC headquarters for all of Europe?"

"PETSEC Europe? No, that's located in Brussels, just across the North Sea. This is the HQ for PETSEC UK, the local branch of the larger European operation. Although that may be changin' pretty soon."

"Oh?" I ask. "And why's that?"

Before Dodger can answer the elevator comes to a quick stop and the door whooshes open, leading us into a well-lit and expensive-looking reception area. Sitting at a desk in front of us is a well-manicured Afghan hound, kind of like my old friend Madame LuLu back in Chicago, except this Afghan is much, much younger and a whole lot better looking. I suck in my gut a little without thinking. Hey, you never know.

"Mornin', Moneypenny," Dodger says, giving her an impish little grin. For some reason that doesn't set well with me, but I decide to let it slide.

"Morning, Dodger, Moose," she answers toothily herself. She shakes her shapely muzzle in the direction of the door right behind her. "Go on in. She's expecting you."

"Thanks," Dodger says, then leans in a little closer. "By the way, you have any plans for later—"

"Oh Dodger, you flirt!" she answers, pushing him back with one paw. "You know I have a boyfriend."

"Never 'urts to ask, though , does it?"

Dodger is standing between me and the door to M's office, so I give him a little shove of my own to get him moving. He opens the door and struts though it without ever taking his eyes off the Afghan. I can't say I really blame him, though. She is a real good looker.

I can't really say the same about M, though. She has medium-length white fur with a long, sad face, droopy jowls and brownish ears that hang well below her muzzle. I think somewhere at some point someone told me she's a Clumber Spaniel, a hunting dog of some sort, but it's pretty clear from one quick look at her that any hunting she might have done is now well in her distant past. If ever it even was a thing for her. Maybe hunting for her dentures, though.

M is sitting at a desk staring at a large computer screen. There are two chairs laid out on this side of the desk, so I pick one and hop on up so I can see over the top of her desk. Dodger does the same.

M doesn't look up right away, so I take the opportunity to scope out her office. Off to our right is a window of some sort, looking out over a large park, with what appears to be Barkingham Palace rising up in the distance. I'm confused for just a moment, trying to square that with the fact that we're about twenty stories underground, when suddenly I realize it's all an illusion, just a giant computer screen giving out an amazingly realistic impression that we're several stories aboveground. And several miles away from here, at that. I'm still trying to figure out if it serves some larger purpose, or simply exists to help relieve a little of the claustrophobia of being buried deep underground, when I notice out of the corner of my eye that M has pushed back her keyboard and is looking my way.

"Agent Moose, it's good to finally make your acquaintance. I take it your trip over here from the palace was uneventful?"

I think back on the moment when I first jumped off the boat, thinking I was about to drown in the river and instead almost cracking a few ribs along the way, and smile. "Yeah, piece of cake. Nice digs you got here, by the way. Makes Fat Tony's office back in Chicago look like a rat's nest by comparison." Fat Tony is the street name for Antonio Gattogrosso, at least as far as anyone is the wiser. He's currently the duly elected president of PETSEC Worldwide, thanks primarily to the fact that no one was running against him. And for that he has only one dog to thank, by the way. And that dog would be me. Well, and also one cat, if you want to get technical about it. But like I said, just one dog.

M waves a paw lazily in the air. "Yes, well, it is comfortable, I suppose. But as busy as I am most days, I hardly notice it." She's wearing a pair of glasses hanging on a slender silver chain around her neck, and she pauses to place them on her muzzle, picking up a piece of paper from the desk in front of her, then dropping it and letting the glasses fall down around her neck again. "So, I take it there's no word yet on the whereabouts of our Chief of Station, Miss Ginger?"

"No, boss," Dodger answers before I can even open my mouth. "We followed up on a lead at Victoria Station, someone spotted that Russian twit Vladimir Kitn wanderin' about the place, but 'e up and disappeared before they could even get in a good chin wag with 'im. So we were kind of 'oping you might 'ave an idea or two what 'e was up to."

"Yes, I saw that report, as well. Very disconcerting, for sure. Anytime that rascal is up and about, you can be certain there's mischief afoot."

"You don't think it might 'ave something to do with the whole Pexit thing, do you?" Dodger asks. "After all, there's a new vote being taken on all that this week, and we still don't know where Her Majesty stands on the subject."

95

M suddenly looks thoughtful and begins tapping on her nose with one paw. "Well, that's certainly one possibility. Kitn has been rather friendly with the PM, of late. And if any country could stand to gain by our leaving the EU, it would be Russia. Although China's not far behind. Hmm, let's see if Phineas can shed some light on all that."

She reaches over and hits a button on her desk phone. "Moneypenny, see if you can round up Mr. Phineas for a chat, if you will."

"Yes, m'lady," Moneypenny's voice purrs over the speaker phone, and I'm beginning to wonder if it's possible to have love at first phone call. And that leads me to wander off into other related thoughts, until I suddenly realize M is talking to me.

"...Phineas' father was a member of the IRA, and so—"

"The IRA?" I ask, trying to cover up a bit for my momentary inattention. "You mean he helped people set up retirement accounts? Like a bean counter? I guess that's important, but as for me, I kind of just rely on my humans to—"

"No, Moose," M says in a slightly scolding voice. "The IRA is not a retirement account or any other such nonsense. It's an acronym for the Irish Retriever Army, a terrorist group that was engaged for many years attacking British gundogs and other British loyalists, back during a time they call 'the Troubles.' His father was arrested at some point and put in prison—"

"Where he stayed until the end o' the war," a voice almost directly behind me says, making me jump a bit in surprise. I turn and come face to face with a large and friendly looking dog with some kind of flat plaid beanie on his head. His long fur is completely red, a much brighter shade than the rather dullish red the lab rats died Bella to match the missing Ginger. He catches my eye and doffs his cap in my direction. "Top o' the' mornin' to ya," he offers. "You must be the famous American agent I've been hearin' all about."

"It's Moose," I answer back. "Moose McGillicutty."

"And a fine Irish name, at that! Well, the McGillicutty part, at least. Can't say nothin' about the Moose bit."

I nod. I really can't say much about the Moose bit either. It's been like a noose around my neck my whole life, other dogs and even stray cats always snickering away about it behind my back, but hey, it's not like we name ourselves, you know? But I'm getting a little off track again, so I think back. What were we talking about? Oh, yeah. "M was telling us about your father," I suggest.

"Oh, right. He spent almost my entire childhood in that stinkin' British prison. The ordeal almost put me sainted mother in an early grave, it did. But then the Brits and the Irish came to an understanding, and they finally let him go."

"Yeah, that had to be rough. I had a buddy got stuck in prison about a year or so back. He was facing the death penalty, but luckily we were able to spring him out in time."

"Ah, yes, laddie, the Southside Prison caper, out in Chicago. A fine Irish town, that." He pronounced "Southside" like it was spelled "South-sayed", but I could pretty much follow along with him despite his accent. And you really can't not like a fellow that has nothing but good to say about your family and your hometown.

M is speaking again, so I perk up my ears to catch it. "—wondering if you could fill us in on what's going on with Pexit and Barkus Johansen."

At the mention of the name Barkus Johansen, Phineas narrows his eyes slightly and I can see one of his canines showing under a raised upper lip. "Johansen, that's a dog what would sell his own mother down the river if it bought him a bone. Or just got him on the telly, for that matter. And as for Pexit, don't even get me started on that. Pulling PETSEC UK out of the EU, that's a fool's errand if there ever was one. And a move that promises to undo all of the gains we've made between England and Northern Ireland ever since the Troubles ended. There's simply no good that can come from that, no good at all."

"So why is anyone supporting it?" I ask, still struggling to figure out what Pug Sit even means, and how one of those flat nosed dogs could possibly fit into Ginger's mysterious disappearance.

M leans in to answer. "How does anything in the world make any sense, these days? At some level, I guess it's all about unbridled nationalism, an England first mentality in our case. And the sudden influx of immigrants who have almost no real understanding of British traditions and customs, that's the icing on the cake. I mean, most of those people have absolutely no idea why it is imperative that everyone queue up and board the buses and trains in a right orderly manner, instead of putting on a mad crush every time a train pulls into an underground station. I don't know if you've noticed, Moose, but the bobbies now have to seal off the entrances to a large percentage of our Tube stations at rush hour, just to keep anyone from getting injured by the overcrowded, uncontrollable mob scene. It's positively barbaric!"

Dodger and Phineas are bobbing their heads in agreement, and I can tell this Pug Sit stuff is a whole lot more popular than they have been suggesting up to this point. I decide to return us to the main topic.

"Tell me more about this Barkus Johansen fellow. What's he all about, and how exactly is he connected to Vladimir Kitn?"

Phineas has had a faraway look in his eyes the whole time M was talking, but now his face clears and he gets back down to the business at paw. "Barkus? Well, for starters, if there ever was a dog that was better named, I don't know who it would be. The guy just never shuts up, just goes waggin' on nonstop about anything and everything, never happy unless he's the center of every conversation and every eye in the room is on him. A perfect example of a Dandie Dinmont terrier, for sure, right down to that wild mane of hair on top o' his head. He's not the full shilling, if you get my drift. Not by a long shot. But he'd tell you otherwise, for certain."

"And so what's his connection with Kitn?" I ask again, trying to move this all along a bit faster.

Phineas shakes his head. "Other than the fact that they are both flat-out Dandies? I don't rightly know for certain. There's no suggestion that Barkus is anything but 100 percent pro-Britain, strange as his ideas might be, but maybe he thinks he can use Kitn for leverage somehow. Or, given the way Parliament has consistently swatted down all of his proposals so far, maybe he just appreciates the unique advantages of being an absolute despot. Rather like the bully on the playground, do it my way or else. No need for any other kind of inducement but sheer brawn. Not that he really has much of that, mind you. Rather a scrawny one, he is, to be sure."

Dodger snorts at that. "A bully? More like a right plonker, I'd say." I'm not really sure what that is, but Phineas seems to be agreeing with him, and M has got one paw clutched in front of her mouth. A paw that doesn't quite cover her smiling eyes.

"Okay," I say, trying to get us all back on track. We've got a dognapping to solve, after all. And the clock is ticking. "Can you think of any reason, any reason at all, why either Barkus Johansen or Vladimir Kitn would want to dognap Ginger?"

Phineas snaps to attention at that. "Ginger? Dognapped? Why wasn't I told? When did this happen?"

M gives me a look that could have killed a lesser dog, and then slowly lays out to Phineas what we know about the situation. Which isn't much.

Phineas is now staring at me with a much more serious look. "So that explains why we've had to enlist the aid of the famous American agent. Yes, it all makes perfect sense, now. And, focusing in on your question, Agent Moose, I think both Johansen and Kitn could benefit greatly by destabilizing the palace somehow. I would assume that you have all paws on deck at the moment, searching for her all across London?" M and I give him a solemn nod. "Well, without Ginger making the rounds and keeping everything and everyone in line, the opportunities for various and assorted mischief go right through the roof, now don't they?"

"We do have a stand-in Corgi in place," I suggest rather weakly.

"And I suppose that's better than nothing. I take it you somehow found another undocked, red-headed Corgi—"

The three of us nod yes. And I have to think that couldn't possibly have been an easy task.

Phineas is looking off in the distance, lost in his thoughts. "Okay, that should slow any perpetrator down for the moment, although with every minute that passes, the risk grows larger." He turns his eyes toward M with a frown. "When is the Queen expected back from Windsor?"

"Tomorrow night," she says, sharing a worried look of her own.

"Great. Just brilliant. And I assume General Mountbatten is at his post upstairs, and not at the palace. Will he be remaining here for the duration of the emergency?"

M nods again.

"Well, in that case, I must be off to the palace meself right away. To take command of the search efforts there, before someone makes a right bags of the whole situation." He starts toward the door, then suddenly pulls up short and turns to me. "But I think you've got a good handle on things, me lad. Vladimir Kitn is in the wind, from what I hear, but Barkus Johansen is your next best shot. I understand 'e's 'aving a do this morning out in front of Downing Street, prancin' about in front of the press corps like a right git, and if you leg it you can probably just catch 'im. Otherwise, even with our 'elp you'd 'ave a mighty fuss and bother trying to get through 'is security. We're not exactly on 'is invite list these days, you know."

"Thanks," I say to his now-retreating back. I check with M, who is giving me what I think is a thumbs up sign (something that is actually quite difficult to pull off without an actual thumb), so I grab Dodger by the shoulder lightly and pull him in the direction of the door. "Okay, Dodge, time to make with the whole native guide thing again. What's the quickest way to get to Downy Street? And please don't tell me we have to take another boat ride!"

The Tower

Thankfully the quickest and easiest way out of the tower is by crossing over on the second floor down from street level, then taking a flight of steps up to the surface. That brings us out well past the tower itself, and into the back of the line of ticket booths stretched out in front.

Nobody seems to notice as we duck out the side door and race across the pavement toward the Tube station. At the very last minute, though, Dodger switches directions on the fly and jumps on board a double-decker bus that is just preparing to pull away from the stop. I barely make it on board myself as the doors slam closed, and am about ready to cuff Dodger about the ears for almost leaving me behind when a big African American man suddenly kneels down in front us. Or do they call them African Englanders over here? I'll have to remember to ask Dodger about that later. But meanwhile, back to the big guy.

"Oh, ho, and what do we have here?" the man says to us in broken but serviceable American Doglish. "Dodger, who's your little buddy?"

"Sweet Chocolate! Just the guy I was looking for!" Dodger motions in my direction with his muzzle. "Hey, Trini, meet Moose. He's from across the pond, just like you."

Trini sticks out a hand and rubs me behind the ears, just like he's known me all my life. That's a bit forward of him, if you ask me, but I have to admit he knows what he's doing with the ears and all. And yes, definitely a fellow American.

"Nice to meet you, Moose," he says, continuing to rub that really special spot that almost gets my rear leg to twitching.

"Uh, nice to meet you back, I guess. But—"

"Uh-huh, you want to know how I happened to learn Doglish, when hardly any other human knows it even exists? Yeah, well that's a long story, my friend, involving this little pit bull I knew back in San Francisco when I was a cable car conductor. She was a real sweety, though, I'll give you that much. Almost broke my heart, she did."

Pit bull? Well, other than Bella, my best friend in the whole world is a pit bull. Killer is his name. Unfortunately so, as it turned out, because he got himself framed for the brutal murder of his girlfriend, a French poodle named Penny. In fact, that's how I got involved in this secret agent business in the first place, trying to figure out who killed Penny and then bust my buddy out of prison. But that's a story for another day. Right now, any friend of a pit bull is a friend of mine, I figure. Especially if he knows how to rub an ear.

Dodger is talking. "—so you see, we need to make it to Downing Street on the double. Think you can 'elp us out?"

"Oh, sure, not a problem. Give me a second." Trini stands up and heads to the front of the bus to talk to the driver. In just a few seconds I see him pick up a small microphone that's attached to the dashboard of the bus and start speaking, this time in regular human English.

"Sorry, folks, but we have a slight detour to make. It seems the police have our roadway blocked off at the moment for some reason. It will only delay us a few minutes, but for anyone who would like to get off and try another form of transportation, we'll be stopping momentarily at the next stop to let you off. Once again, we apologize for any inconvenience this might cause." With that he winks broadly in our direction, and after a short stop during which just a few riders jump off, we are quickly on our way. Downy Street here we come!

9 1/2 Downing Street

When the bus finally pulls up in front of Johansen's residence at 9 1/2 Downy Street, I can see that a sizable crowd of reporters has already formed up inside the gates, and someone—Johansen, I presume—is standing in front of a makeshift lectern of some kind, talking. Among all the usual animal reporters is a small cluster of humans, standing around with their notepads out looking totally confused. The residence itself is heavily guarded by a large police contingent, and as we trot up to the gates they make a tentative move to stop us, then one of the coppers sees my blue collar and waves us on through.

Johansen is some kind of terrier, all right, a little heavier than me but with the same short legs and a funny tangle of blond hair sticking straight up out of the top of his head. He looks kind of like his mistress took him to the cut-rate groomers and they missed a big spot right on top. But for what it's worth, he doesn't seem to notice, and he's holding court before the reporters with great enthusiasm. Dodger and I edge in among all the legs to try and listen in. Some canine reporter has just asked him a question, and he dives into the answer with no hesitation, kind of like I attack a big bowl of kibble.

"Good question," he says, although his face is saying otherwise. "But let me ask you, where would England be today if our greatest leaders took that attitude? Take Neville Chamberland, for example, the Great Appeaser. If Winston Churchill hadn't pushed him aside, we'd probably all be speaking fluent German right about now. And after Churchill won the war for us, what did we do to thank him for his service? Why, we kicked him right out the door, the same door that's standing right behind me now." He stops and points toward a large human door that's marked with the number 10. Beside it is a matching black doggie door marked 9 ½. Johansen turns back to face the reporters. "We kicked our Churchill out and replaced him with another appeaser, a globalist, and where did that get us? Before you know it we're so weak even Argentina was kicking us around, and the rest of the world was betting good money that the Argies would end up kicking us right in the arse. Imagine that, bloody England, Queen of the High Seas, getting kicked around by a two-bit banana republic! But we didn't get boofed, now, did we? And you know why? Because we had Margaret Thatcher, The Iron Lady, that's why. We finally had a leader once again with more rigid steel in her backbone than the forges of Sheffield has ever produced, a leader England rightly deserved. No Elizabeth May, that one, not by a long shot. And with Thatcher at the helm, the Falklands War was over in just ten weeks, and England was back in its proper station in the world." He pauses and takes a sip from a glass of water perched on the edge of his podium, then starts up again, almost without taking a breath.

"And with Britannia back in full bloom again, once more we turned our back on English Exceptionalism and agreed to join the Useless Union, the very epitome of unexceptionalism, the very model of mediocracy. Here we are, the country that paved the way for modern democracy on the 15th of June, Year of Our Lord 1215, on the verdant fields of Runnymede. The very country that under the leadership of Sir Francis Drake single-handedly sunk the Spanish fleet in 1588, giving us unquestioned mastery of the entire world. The very country that stood bravely and stoically against the Germans in 1940 and 1941 when every other country in Europe had caved without even a hint of a fight. Our England, bearing unthinkable losses to the Luftwaffe and the German V-2s with our chins held up high, biding time until the Americans could finally come to their senses and use our island as a launching point to take the war to Hitler's doorstep. And now those very Europeans who invited Hitler into their homes eighty years ago, who fed the Nazis and sheltered them while they plotted the brutal destruction of our beloved island, they want nothing less than to destroy once more everything that is glorious about our English culture and our English way of life. They want us to house and feed the broken rejects of their own failed economic policy. They want us to prostrate ourselves before a runaway socialist scheme where even the right to basic agriculture and innovation is governed by a bureaucratic state, a committee that allocates such things to this country or that according to the wanton dictates of the fat, indolent lobbyists in Brussels. And my friends, it is all too clear why that is so. Our beloved England has long been the envy of a destitute and despicable Europe. Of the French, who would rather work one day a week and complain bitterly the other six about their lot in life. Of the

Greeks, who schemed illegally to undermine the European currency, and now refuse to pay the price for their crimes. Or the Germans, who secretly pine for a return to their glory years, and see the EU as nothing less than a path to world conquest by other means. No, my England is not going to fall victim to these sordid plots, my England is not going to let itself be trampled underfoot by our wantonly craven brothers and sisters from across the North Sea. England has remained firm as an island fortress for almost one thousand years now, jealously guarding her borders and beating back any and all invaders, including the Nazis, and we will not weaken our resolve today. God Save the Queen, I say, and God Save Canine Britannia!"

"But, but, what about the trade issues?" splutters one reporter near the front of the crowd. "What about the border with Northern Ireland?"

"What about them?" Barkus shouts back defiantly. "We made our peace with Northern Ireland long before PETSEC EU came along, and we will do so again! And as for imports and exports, any difference between being either in or out of their Union is completely artificial, now, isn't it? If the French want to sell us their wine, or the Greeks their olives,

113

then they'll just figure out a way to do so, now won't they? And if they want to taste the produce from our magnificent English farms, then they'll work out how to expedite our fruits and vegetables across the border, just as it's done now. The idea that any of that is going to change in any material way is pure poppycock, a baseless arse-over-backwards argument intended only to confuse the real issue at stake here, their plan to break England's back and subject us to the same confiscatory taxation and regulatory scheme that has kept the people of Europe in the thrall of the billionaire class, that has shackled innovation and creativity lest it lend its fertile soil to the seeds of burgeoning individuality and rebellion! Since time immemorial our England has always been the birthplace of mankind's greatest achievements, of democracy and art and finance and all manner of things that have sparked the rise of humanity and freed us from the artificial limits imposed by those whose vested interests have always found refuge in the overworked soil of our past. Pexit is nothing more than the next step in that long journey, an indispensable guarantee that England will continue to govern her own glorious destiny, unbridled by the greedy, small-minded gnomes that hold sway over Europe. Gnomes that have kept Europe captive in their tight-fisted, malevolent grip. But not so our England, not now, I say. Hail Pexit, ladies and gentlemen! Hail liberty! Hail Britannia!"

The whole time he's been talking his hair has been flopping around in the wind like some kind of a wild animal, almost in perfect sync with his pumping fist, adding a kind of hypnotic rhythm to his words. He's turning to leave now, holding up one hand to ward off any further questions from the crowd, obviously sensing that he's won them over and saying anything more will just water down the wave of enthusiasm and encouragement that has washed over all of us who are watching. As for me, I'm kind of just standing here, stunned, when suddenly Dodger grabs my shoulder and pulls me forward through the crowd.

"Come on, Moose, we've got to catch 'im before 'e gets away!"

Luckily the rest of the crowd seems to be just as stunned as I am, and we easily wiggle our way through the sea of ankles and calves, bursting through the front and then past the security detail. In just a handful of moments we've worked our way to the jet black front door of 9 ½ Downy Street, and are waiting for Johansen when he walks up.

I'm busy searching around for something, anything to get his autograph when Dodger swats me across my ears. "Pay attention, Moose! We don't 'ave much time!"

"Well, then, what have we got here?" a voice calls out, surprising me.

I look up from scrounging for a scrap of paper on the ground and find that Johansen is standing right in front of me. With his short legs, we're almost muzzle-to-muzzle, and I suddenly realize that during his speech he must have been squatting on some kind of elevated platform. That only makes sense, I guess. Makes it easier for everyone to see you.

While I'm just standing there, star struck, Dodger shoulders me aside and steps up to confront Johansen dog-to-dog.

"Mr. Johansen, allow me to introduce meself. The name is Dodger, and this is Agent Moose, the rather famous secret agent from across the pond. We've been sent here from PETSEC HQ to ask you a few questions, if you don't mind."

Johansen waves him off with a brusque paw. "I'm afraid I do mind, my good fellow. I'm terribly busy at the moment, you know. If you wish to speak to me, please make arrangements with my secretary. I'm sure she can squeeze in a minute or two out of my schedule over the next week or so. And now, please to chivvy along, now, would you?"

He makes to brush past us, but Dodger holds his ground. Johansen's security detail looks like it's ready to step in at any moment, but they keep eyeing my blue collar, and it's set them to talking angrily amongst themselves for some reason. Boy, if I'd only known a simple little blue collar could have this much impact on people, I'd have been wearing one a long time ago, I promise you!

Meanwhile. Dodger is apparently not letting up on Barkus Johansen.

"Mr. Johansen, I know you've 'ad secret meetings with the Russian, Vladimir Kitn, and I simply need to know exactly what was discussed in those meetings."

Secret meetings with Kitn? That's the first I've heard of that—

Johansen is scowling and shaking his head. "I assure you, I have absolutely no idea what you're talking about, my good fellow. Now be off with you before I have you arrested."

I can see that the security guards have finally made up their minds about the whole blue collar thing, and several of them are already bringing out pawcuffs, so I jiggle Dodger to get his attention.

"Time to make like a tree and bug out of here," I tell him in no uncertain terms.

Johansen has used the diversion to slide past us and is already disappearing through the small doggie door, so I grab Dodger's collar and steer him in the opposite direction of Johansen's muscle. In seconds we've made it through the few remaining reporters and are high-tailing it to safety. Well, at least Dodger's high-tailing it. My bobbed tail is more like short-tailing it.

When we've finally made it across the street to the shade of a small clutch of trees, I turn on Dodger with undisguised fury.

"Well, that really accomplished a lot," I tell him angrily. "Now all you've done is make an enemy out of him. And such a brilliant, insightful dog, at that!"

"Wut? Brilliant, you say? You mean you actually bought into all that boloney of 'is?" Dodger is looking at me like I've lost my mind. "The dog is right starkers, I tell you. English Exceptionalism? Hah! Now 'e's got the mobs thinkin' like a bunch of mud-brained Americans." He pauses. "Present company excepted, of course," he adds, although I'm not really buying any of his apology.

"Yeah, well, you gotta admit he's got a good point about freedom and independence, about not being chained to all of Europe's failed ideas. After all, that's the kind of patriotic thinking that's making America great again."

Dodger looks disgusted. "And you really think that turnin' your backs on anyone who looks or acts or believes differently from you is the answer? That bigotry really makes you great?"

"Well, it beats—" I start to offer in my defense.

"Humph. And do you really think your America would 'ave ever been all that great in the first place if you 'adn't put aside your differences as individual states and formed one united, unified country? Look at your own 'istory, after all, the way your country almost completely failed before you finally set aside your first attempt at a constitution and replaced it with one that weakened the powers of each of the individual states. Oh, I'm sorry, I forgot, you Americans don't spend all that much time studying 'istory. The truth is all too inconvenient, after all. And fake news is such a convenient alternative"

"But I—"

"We got a really good deal going 'ere, you see, all the benefits of EU membership with almost none of the downside, and now tossers like Johansen want to muck it all up for the rest of us. I guess it just takes one bloomin' bad apple to spoil it for the rest of us, you know?"

Dodger's rantings are starting to make my ears hot, but somehow I can't seem to come up with any good arguments to prove him wrong. I guess all my best oral talents are concentrated on eating. But that doesn't change my first good point.

"Okay, Mr. Smarty Pants, but even if you're right, that still doesn't change the fact that we didn't manage to accomplish a single thing with our meeting today. Now he's mad at us, and anything we could ever hope to get out of him about the Russians and their secret plans is lost in the wind as well."

"No, Moose, that's where you're wrong." Dodger reaches into a little fur-colored pouch he's carrying across his shoulders and pulls out a small square-shaped device with a screen kind of like what you'd see on a cell phone. "While I was busy distractin' Johansen with my demands, secretly I was plantin' a small trackin' device on 'im. There was no way 'e was ever going to admit to meetin' up with the Russians, but now we can keep close tabs on 'im goin' forward—"

"And catch him in the act when he does! That's absolutely genius, Dodger!"

"Well, yes, I'll 'ave to admit it was a bit genius," Dodger says, his muzzle turning a bright shade of red underneath his fur. "But what's even better is, the tracker broadcasts everythin' being said in anywhere in the vicinity of it back to a listenin' post at the Tower. If he's up to somethin'—and I've got to believe a git like that'n is up to his smarmy sleeves in somethin' rather nasty—then that'll be our best chance of catchin' the bloke with the bloody 'ook still hangin' from 'is mouth."

121

I have to admit I wish I'd thought of that myself. And now, it seems, our clever little Mr. Johansen doesn't seem quite so clever to me, after all.

Outside Parliament

With no particular game plan in place at the moment, we're trotting along a big wide street with lots of solid-looking stone and brick buildings stretching out in almost every direction. There's a man selling flowers out of a small wagon about a block in front of us, and with my nose already starting to twitch from all the pollen, I gesture to Dodger and cross the street, keeping one wary eye on the flower vendor the whole time. Those guys have a bad habit of chasing you down like a fox taking down a scared rabbit, trying to guilt you into buying a bunch of roses for your girlfriend or wife. Or both. Pure evil, I tell you. Absolutely diabolical.

We manage to pass the flower guy with no major incidents, though, so my threat status is back to code yellow. Dodger has suggested we try to find a nearby Tube station to hang out in, ready to roll the moment some news pops up about Johansen or Kitn. Or, better yet, both. Since I don't have any better ideas at the moment, and since we currently have no leads on the missing Corgi, that plan makes pretty good sense to me, I reckon.

With Dodger taking the lead, we've just passed a restaurant of some sort that calls itself The Red Lion, and the smells coming out of its kitchen are making my stomach rumble something fierce. There's a giant clock tower looming just above our heads, and when I look up, I can see it's already way past noon. Okay, yeah, I usually only get fed twice a day, but then I almost never take a walkie all over the city of London, either. So it's only natural I might be getting a little hungry right about now.

"Hey, Dodger, what do you think about trying to rustle up some grub around here?" I ask, rubbing my belly a little to make my point.

Dodger looks back at me with a slight frown. "Rustle up some grub worms? Oh, I'm sure we can do much better than that! But you're right, I'm a bit Hank Marvin meself, now that I think about it." He looks around, spotting The Red Lion, then glances back at the large brown building underneath the clock tower. "Well, we could nip into a chippy, I suppose, but they'd be highly unlikely to serve us. Or appreciate our even being in there in the first place, being that we're dogs and all. No, our best bet is probably the cafeteria in Parliament. Your collar is bound to be worth something in there."

He turns on his heel and starts trotting toward the brown building, and I follow right behind. Once inside, he leads me along an endless series of hallways and stairs, and it isn't long before the enticing odor of freshly cooked food is marching happily through my nostrils.

"Here we are," Dodger says abruptly, standing in front of a rather plain-looking door, with no restaurant anywhere in sight. He sees my confusion and leans in to whisper to me conspiratorially. "This 'ere is the back door to the kitchen. Much less likely to draw unwanted attention to our comings and goings, am I right?"

I have to admit that secrecy is the very essence of a spy's life, so he's got a good point there. But the door is closed, and Dodger's just sitting there staring at it like something's supposed to happen. I'm just about to ask him what's he's waiting for when suddenly the door slams open and this big fellow with an all-white outfit and apron comes barreling out, a full-to-almost-overflowing black trash bag clutched in each hand. He doesn't seem to notice us as he hauls the trash down the hall toward the back exit, and Dodger and I take that golden opportunity to dive through the door before it slams closed behind us.

Once inside, the kitchen turns out to be a regular symphony of sights, sounds and smells. Pots are being slung onto stovetops, plates and silverware dumped into sinks, and waiters and cooks are scurrying about madly in almost every direction. The only thing I don't see is a menu or a place for us to sit, but once again Dodger seems to have that all worked out.

"Watch and learn, Moose," he tells me with a wink, then without another word he scoots over to where the cleanup crew is emptying uneaten food off of plates and into a series of large trash cans. "Our feast awaits," he grins, positioning himself right beside one of the cans as I quickly follow suit.

One of the cleanup guys spots us immediately. "Aw, look at you, you cheeky little buggers. I bet you want something to get you through the day, prolly 'aven't eaten in a week, am I right? Well, then, 'ere you go." He grabs a plate in each hand and shoves them underneath a table, well out of the way of the traffic, then turns back to his work.

Dodger seems to have made out with a pasta dish of some sort, while I've got the remains of a boneless pork chop with a bit of dressing and green peas on the side. I don't have to be told twice what my next move is, and I can see out of the corner of my eye that Dodger's got the same idea. In less than a minute I'm licking my plate clean, ready for it to go back on the shelf, all the while glancing over at Dodger's plate to make sure he hasn't left a choice morsel or two behind. Which he hasn't, of course. Now that we're all done, our benefactor reaches down and snatches up our plates with a smile.

"Clean as a whistle," he laughs, laying the plates on top of a stack he's already scraped. "Why, I need you two to come along more often. Makes my job a whole lot easier!"

With that he grabs the plates and hauls them over to the dishwashers just a few feet away, leaving us to lean back and let out a few top-quality burps. I guess we should have gone ahead and split, but after a fine meal like that, a fellow just needs to sit back and savor it for a moment.

"So what's the deal with that Trini fellow?" I ask Dodger, mostly just trying to pass the time before we have to leave for the Tube station.

Dodger glances my way with a big smile plastered across his puss. "Sweet Chocolate? Oh, 'e's a fine one, that one is. Came to London a few years back, 'e did. Seems 'is pit bull, a lovely lady named Sara, she 'ad a rare type of illness that only this one veterinarian in England knew 'ow to treat. So Trini left 'is job working the cable cars in San Francisco and brought 'er 'ere. Stayed with 'er at the 'ospital almost night and day, until she finally passed on. A sad story, that."

It was a sad little story, and I have to blink back a small tear that's starting to gather strength in my left eye. I've never had to deal all that much with losing someone, other than that one time with Killer's girlfriend, and even then I didn't know her all that well. But still, even knowing all the good dogs go to heaven, it kind of breaks your heart whenever any dog has to make that trip.

But something else is still confusing me. "Okay, but how is it Trini figured out how to speak Doglish? I've never heard of any other human who was that intelligent. They usually all sound like a bunch of halfwit apes at a banana convention."

"Hmm. Yes." Dodger is busy eyeing all the action in the kitchen, and he seems to be coming to the conclusion that we might be close to overstaying our welcome. But he still risks a few more minutes to finish the story for me. "Well, as I understand it, the whole time Trini was lying there next to Sara, 'e was talking to 'er, trying to give 'er the strength to get through it all, one way or the other. And in the meantime, she started talking back to 'im. Back and forth they went, over and over, and finally it started to sink in to 'im that she was actually saying something. Over time, 'e started figuring out all the nuances of 'er barks and growls, I guess. And her whines, of course, given the pain she was in. Once 'e made it past that hurdle, the rest was easy, and before you know it, he could speak Doglish almost as well as a puppy." Dodger laughed. "Well, not the Queen's Doglish, of course. American Doglish, mostly, which only makes sense, since 'e learned it from an American dog."

"So he learned proper Doglish, you're saying," I suggest.

"Proper? Oh, there's nothing at all proper about American Doglish. You colonists 'ave right butchered the language, you 'ave, to the point where it's sometimes 'ard to even understand what you're saying. What is it they say, we're just two people separated by a common language? Well, I don't know about that, but if anything's at all common, it would be your completely pretzeled American version of the Queen's own Doglish, that's for certain."

I'm about to take exception to that comment when Dodger wags his nose sharply behind me, and as I turn my head to check over my shoulder I can see a fat, mean-looking cook with a tall white hat heading our way.

"That's the 'ead chef," Dodger warns me, jumping to his feet. "I think 'e wants us to pay up and leave. Chop chop."

With our stomachs now full, half the day behind us and the mystery of Ginger's whereabouts still in front of us, I'll have to agree with Dodger on this one—having a conversation with a tall, scowling human who's just grabbed a meat cleaver off a chopping block he's passing—his eyes boring murderously into mine—well, that can probably wait for another day. Someone's just hauling another load of trash out the back door, and Dodger and I take quick advantage of our good luck and hit the streets before Cheffy back there can hit us with something else. And something sharp and highly unpleasant, at that.

Outside, I check the clock again. Just past one in the afternoon, it says. "Hey Dodge, is that thing accurate?" I ask, pointing up at the clock.

"Big Ben?" he answers with a scowl. "Why, it's as right as rain, and as trustworthy as jolly old England herself. But I get your point. It's getting rather late in the day, an' we still 'aven't seen 'ide nor 'air of Ginger."

Given the distinct possibility that whoever dognapped Ginger hasn't been exactly kind to her for the duration, I would have probably used a very different phrase to describe the situation. But I get his point. We are, after all, the lead agents in the investigation, and so far we have little or nothing to show for it. For all we've accomplished, we might as well be hanging back at the palace like Bella, lounging around on soft pillows and eating bon bons off a silver platter, living the life of Reilly. But for the life of me,

I've got bupkis when it comes to ideas on where to head next. Or what to do when we get there.

"So, where do we go now?" I ask, looking up and down the street and seeing nothing that appears at all helpful.

Dodger is glancing around, as well. "Hmm. Just about any direction right now is equally useless to us. So I might suggest we 'ead down to Westminster Underground. That way, as soon as we 'ear something from the tracker I placed on Johansen we can 'op a train to pretty much anywhere in the city."

"Well, you're the native guide," I reply, "so lead on, Tonto." As we turn to head off down the street, I check once more to make sure the blue collar is still working. Until we hear something more from Q'ute's sneaky little ears or M's network of spies, we're lying about as dead in the water as I thought I was going to be when we jumped off the ferry boat just a few hours ago. My legs are killing me from all the walking, and I can't help but think back again on Bella, taking it easy back at the palace. Just for once I wonder why I can't play the decoy for a change, instead of racing all around the city chasing shadows and getting chased in turn by fat men bearing large sharp knives. She certainly drew the plum assignment, that's for sure.

Bella

Barkingham Palace

A girl could really get used to this kind of life, I'm here to tell you. A million different but equally luxurious places to take a long, uninterrupted nappie, and all the food and drink you could ever want literally just a paw wave away. Throw in some good belly rubs and I'm not sure they'll ever get me out of this place. It's sort of like being a Disney princess for a day. But of course, that kind of makes sense, doesn't it, since the whole point of the palace is to house and pamper real human princesses. And princes.

I have no idea what Moose is up to, but at least he has that feisty little dog Dodger around to keep him out of trouble, so for the moment I'm not going to worry about him. In the meantime, I'll have to admit that I'm getting a little bit bored—believe it or not, there's only so many nappies a girl can take in one day, and over the years I've gotten pretty used to Moose stirring up some kind of nonsense or other back in the old neighborhood. Or more lately, back at the marina.

With nothing else to do around here, a short walk around the palace seems like a pretty swell idea. I don't have to really worry about getting lost, because one set of rooms is every bit as good as any other set of rooms, at least as far as I'm concerned. Just endless acres of thickly padded carpet and thousands of pictures of dead people. You'd think even the humans would get bored with all that at some point.

I've just stepped into a hallway that seems to stretch away forever and am trying to decide whether to turn to the left or the right when I notice one of the Queen's guards with those tall furry hats staring pointedly in my direction, about twenty feet off to my left. After a long moment, during which a full range of emotions seem to flash across his face, he finally decides to say something.

"Ginger? Is that you? What the—"

It takes me another long moment to process it all, the idea that somehow he thinks I'm Ginger. But then of course he does! That was the whole point of my being here in the first place, right? The palace staff haven't given me any real instructions on how I'm supposed to react to this sort of thing, so I just go with my own gut instincts and wag my tail at him once or twice. After all, that's what I do when my mistress Helen calls me Bella, and Ginger and I can't be all that different deep inside. Even if she is royalty.

Evidently the tail wag is dead on point, because the guard appears convinced that I'm the real deal. He immediately reaches into his pocket and fishes out a cell phone—one of the old timey phones, a flip phone I think they call it—and starts punching something in. I can hear ringing on the other end, then somebody answering it, but I can't make out much of anything from that end. This side of the conversation, however, is crystal clear.

"Ivan, you won't believe it! Ginger is back!" He pauses while the other person mumbles something. "I know, I know, but I'm standing here staring at the dog right this moment. Long tail, red fur, a Corgi—it's Ginger all right! I thought you had her locked away good. You fool! How in world did you let her escape, especially given how hard it was to capture that *собака* in first place?" Another set of mumbles. "Okay, go look, but I'm telling you, I know at what I'm looking, and it's Ginger for sure!"

Cursing to himself, he flips the phone shut and shoves it back into his pocket, then starts walking slowly in my direction with a determined, angry look on his face. As he gets closer, though, his face goes slack, and he gets down on one knee, beckoning toward me.

"Here, little doggie. Come here. Ginger want a treat? Ginger want a doggie bone?"

When I don't move, he gets up again and comes closer, talking to me in that little human puppy language they seem to think works for us dogs. But of course it doesn't. I mean, they wouldn't try that trick with another adult human, now would they? And dogs, as you well know, are so much more sophisticated than stupid humans.

When he finally gets within a few feet of me, he sticks out one hand like maybe he's got a treat in it to offer me, although I can tell by the smell he's empty handed. I guess I should have taken off at a full run the very first instant he started in with all of this, but clearly this guard is the one solitary lead we have on what's happened to Ginger. I mean, he recognized me on sight—sort of—and then phoned a friend, who evidently has Ginger locked away somewhere safe. And that's good news for now, I suppose, the news that's she's still alive. Although in what condition is anyone's guess at this point.

As the guard bends closer, reaching out toward me with that one hand, I'm trying desperately to drum up some plan of action, some way to alert the authorities to what I've just found out, but I'm coming up completely blank. And I can't even get a good read on his face to recognize him in a police lineup later on—to be honest, other than the handful of humans I deal with on a regular basis, and other than obvious differences like skin color and gender, one random human looks pretty much like any other human to me. This one is white, male, and that's basically all I got. A good description for probably ninety percent of the Queen's guards at the palace. Or more, now that I think about it.

But then I catch it, a whiff of something exotic, something I've never smelled before, but it's gone before I can manage to process the smell any further. That does manage to distract me, though, and almost before I know it he's lunging straight toward me, trying to grab my collar! His fingers start to close in on my ruff even as I kick my short little Corgi legs into high gear, shooting right between his legs for the open door at the far end of the hallway!

I'm barking my brains out, calling for backup, and he's right on my tail screaming at me in some foreign language I can't place. And I've got to give it to him, for a human this guy is fast! For once I start to regret my full-size tail, which gives him a great target to grab hold of, so as I run I tuck it up over my back in a tight curl to keep it away from him.

I make it to the door with just a few feet to spare, then shoot off to my left, hoping against hope I don't find myself stuck in a dead end somewhere. Which of course I immediately do. Both of the exit doors to the place are locked, meaning I have to turn back the way I came, somehow still managing to avoid him. The old and well-used phrase "dead end" is starting to take on more sinister and immediate implications.

Luckily I've played this little game a thousand times or more with Moose in the back yard back in Chicago, the old cat-and-mouse-and-dog thing. The key to winning is to remain completely unpredictable in your movements, using misdirection to keep your pursuer constantly guessing about which direction you're going to turn. And it helps that, even though my short legs give up quite a bit in the speed department, being built low to the ground more than makes up for it in terms of agility. I can turn on a dime and give you nine cents change, if you know what I mean. Well, I could if I ever actually carried around any loose change. But, no pockets, you know?

Anyway, having discovered that the second door is locked, I spin around to see my attacker bearing down on me at full speed, hands outstretched to grab me at the first opportunity. This ironically offers up another big advantage for me, as reaching out like that throws his balance off a bit, and I jump on that advantage immediately, racing straight at him before juking left, then right, then left again. He tries to copy my moves, but that only leaves him flailing around out of balance like a drunk uncle at a wedding dance. As I dash past him I plant a solid bite into the boot covering his left ankle, and use my momentum to swing my little Corgi body around behind him, releasing at the last critical minute to land at full speed pointing straight toward the exit door.

After screaming something nasty at me and grabbing at his unfortunately well-protected ankle, he takes off after me once again at full throttle. I've got a good lead on him by now, though, and when I get to the doorway I used when I turned into the hallway the first time, I leap through without a second's hesitation. Since I came through here before I'm pretty sure it's not another dead end, and I can somewhat remember the various twists and turns that got me here to this very spot just a few minutes earlier. I'm only hoping and praying that "somewhat" is good enough to save my little Corgi butt. And I don't really have a lot of margin here.

With the Queen off at her other castle, Barkingham Palace is pretty much deserted, but far off in the distance I'm picking up the sound of several human voices and I head lickety-split in that direction. I'm finally starting to run out of gas, my rear end rabbit kicks starting to stumble a bit in the over-thick carpet, when suddenly I burst through a doorway and run right into one of the Royals, the red-headed one they call Harry, I think. Well, I don't exactly run *into* him, more like around him, and then I pull up short to seek welcome refuge behind the prince's legs, my chest heaving with exhaustion and my heart pounding in my ears. Harry's looking down at me even as I see my pursuer race into the room. Then, as he catches a good eyeful of who I'm with, no less than a prince of the United Kingdom, my mysterious pursuer just as quickly retreats back into the hall. I look up at Harry, my hero.

"Ginger?" Harry's saying to me, reaching down to scratch my head. "You're in a right bit of hurry for a girl your age, now aren't you? What's the matter, old girl? Missing the Queen or something?"

Of course, since the Prince doesn't speak a word of Doglish I can't possibly explain to him what has just happened, but at least I'm safe for now. And of course the head scratch is a big bonus. When I'm sure my attacker is long gone I give the Prince's hand a quick lick and head back into the bowels of the palace, searching for Victoria or anyone else on her staff to warn them about the dognapping guard. And keeping a sharp lookout the whole time for any other co-conspirators who might try to stop me. Or worse.

Barkingham Palace

A fter all the furious racing about here and yonder trying to keep my soft red fur firmly attached to my little Corgi body, the rest of my trip through the palace is a lot slower paced. I have absolutely no idea where I'm headed, but I try to keep my bearings in the general direction of exactly opposite to where I've just been. After all, I may have been born at night, but it wasn't last night. If somebody's out there who's already dognapped the first Ginger and then almost got their mitts on Ginger Number Two, I'm not taking any chances on reprising that particular starring role, believe you me. Instead, I make sure to stick to the edges of every room I pass through, using the furniture, flower pots and well-polished suits of armor to protect me from prying, unfriendly eyes.

In the end, though, all of my efforts to stay furtive proved to be ineffective. And that turns out to be a good thing, because instead of my finding Victoria, she finds me. Or at least one of her people finds me, a female Corgi barely weaned from her mum who is serving an internship at the palace. When I explain quickly what has just transpired, and my theory about the dognapping guard, she immediately guides me through the Byzantine warrens of the palace straight to the Secret Service's communications hub buried deep within the basement, a place I would never have found on my own, not in a million years. Dog years, that is.

When we walk in, Victoria is in the midst of a serious conversation with a dog whose breed I can't say I've ever seen. He has a longish coat, red like mine but much brighter in color, and as soon as he sees me he breaks off his conversation in mid-bark.

"Ah, and what have we here? The ersatz Ginger, I take it. I must say you've done a masterful job with the disguise. As always, Victoria. If I hadn't known better I would have taken her for the real Ginger for sure."

Victoria steps up to introduce us. "Bella, this gentleman's name is Phineas. He joined us here a few years back from our Irish offices. He's a specialist in anti-terrorism, which, as you know, is a growing problem for us here in England, and of particular concern when it comes to protecting the Royal Family."

"Pleased to meet you," I say, sticking out a paw, and he hesitates for but a brief moment, a slow smile spreading across his face as he returns the gesture.

"Pleased to meet you back," he tells me. "And from the accent I gather you and Agent Moose are related?"

"Well, I'm his adopted sister, but we both grew up in the same small town just outside of Chicago. I— I take it you've already met my brother?"

"Oh, yes. I ran into him back at PETSEC's UK headquarters in the Tower of London. And he's got quite an impressive resume, I must say, although it doesn't exactly show in his physical stature."

"What he lacks in size he more than makes up for in pluck," I explain.

Phineas nods, still smiling. "Yes, yes, well that goes without saying." He points to a couple of small cushions and motions for me to take a load off, and after everything that I've just been through I'm more than happy to oblige. He points again toward the door the intern has just disappeared through. "I see you've met little Myrna. Quite a good little dog, that lassie, good head on her shoulders. I'm hoping she will find a permanent home here when her internship is over." He seems to notice the dried saliva on my muzzle, reaching out a paw to examine it. "Land sakes, child, but you look like you've been through a wringer. Is everything okay?"

Quickly I fill Phineas and Victoria in on what I discovered about Ginger's likely dognapper.

As I tell my tale, Phineas is rubbing one paw along the side of his muzzle. "Ivan was the name you heard, eh? The accomplice on the other end of the phone? That's a Russian name, for certain."

"And you say the man chasing you was cursing in some foreign language?" Victoria asks, cutting her eyes toward Phineas. "Could he have been speaking Russian?"

"Well, I can't be sure," I answer uncertainly. "But I know it wasn't a language I recognize, like French, German or Italian. And it clearly wasn't some kind of Asian dialect, or Arabic or even Indian."

Phineas nods "So by the process of elimination I think we've arrived at our answer. It's the Russians, all right, no doubt about it. Particularly given the fact that Vladimir Kitn has now taken up a hopefully temporary residence in our fair city."

That news certainly perks up my ears. "Kitn? Here?" I don't know a whole lot about the cat, but from what Moose has told me in the past, that guy is pure evil.

"Yes," Phineas says, his smile now completely gone. "And your brother Agent Moose is now hot on his tail. With any luck, and given Moose's sterling reputation, we'll have our paws on him well before he can manage to pull off whatever dastardly plan he's cooked up for us."

When they first started talking about Moose being a top-notch secret agent and all, I figured it was all pretty funny, but now the thought of little Moosey going head-to-head with one of the biggest monsters this world has ever seen has got my head spinning.

"Please tell me he's not out there trying to handle this all by himself," I beg them.

Phineas shakes his head. "Oh, no, we'd never let that happen. This city is too big and way too foreign for Agent Moose to handle all of its eccentricities on his own. No, we have him paired up with Dodger. He'll be just fine."

Oh, yeah. Dodger, that little Nor-something terrier we met earlier this morning. "And Dodger, is he some kind of Double-O agent himself?" I ask, feeling a little better about everything now. But just by a little bit.

Victoria laughs. "Double-O? Hardly. Agents like Moose seem to come along but once in a lifetime, if then. No, Dodger is a former felon, I'm afraid, but he's fully reformed now, and seems to have a good handle on every questionable character and every dodgy situation that's afoot on the streets of London. Hence how he got his nickname in the first place. His original name was Bowser, I believe."

Now I'm back to the part where my stomach is doing flip flops and my heart is beating out a rhumba in my chest. Moose is out loose on the mean streets of London trying to track down an evil maniac, and his only possible backup is a reformed ex-con? At least back in Chicago he had Fat Tony, Tommy Tuxedo and a long list of highly reliable friends. I'm just about to express my concerns when Phineas speaks up again.

"I can sense your concern, my lady, but you really shouldn't worry. He's wearing the blue collar, after all, plus ever since the 2005 terrorist attack we have cameras and live assets on almost every street corner in London."

"And yet you say Vladimir Kitn is hiding out somewhere in London but you have no idea where that is," I point out the obvious. "Plus you have had your own chief of station for Barkingham Palace dognapped right out from under your very noses, yet you still have no idea how it happened or where they're currently holding her. Did I get that right?"

Phineas is now looking rather sheepish, which is a pretty neat trick for a dog, and Victoria is pointedly refusing to meet my gaze. "Uh, yeah, that's about the gist of it," he finally spits out, then seems to catch a second wind. "But hey, at least we have a lead on Ginger now, as flimsy as it may seem. You say you probably couldn't pick out the phony guard in a lineup, but we do have two good things to work with. First, you managed to take a good chomp out of the side of his boot as you ran past him. If we can identify one of the guards with a similar type of damage to his boot, then it's almost certain we've pinpointed our man. Second, there's that scent you picked up but can't seem to place. If you can get close enough to the guards that are still here in the palace, maybe you can pick it up again."

Victoria is frowning and staring off into a far corner of the room, apparently thinking everything through. "Assuming, of course, it's not an odor that is common among all the other guards, like a cologne they all like or a lingering smell on one common component of their uniforms," she adds, putting a real downer on what I had hoped was instead a big breakthrough in the case.

Phineas pops back up on all four paws. "Well, we will just have to deal with all that when we get to that point. But for now, according to my timepiece, we're coming up on the changing of the guard. We'll never have a better time to catch them all together, so Ginger—sorry, Bella, it's all so confusing, you know—please come along and we'll see if you can single out your mystery culprit. If we miss this opportunity, we may never have another one—he can just slip away from us sight unseen, and our real Ginger may wind up lost to us forever."

"Oh, my," Victoria exclaims, looking down at her watch. "We haven't a moment to lose! Let's be off right away, shall we?"

Barkingham Palace

When we finally arrive at the parade grounds in front of Barkingham Palace, the Queen's Guards are all lined up in the middle of the field. We've been running the entire time, and I'm completely out of breath again, but I know I need to buck up now and get this done. Ginger is counting on me, after all, and maybe all of England as well. Or at least all of the English pets.

We don't have time to stop and check the left ankles of all of the guards, and I'm not exactly sure how we would manage to pull that off even if we did, so our current go-to plan is for me to race up and down the lines of guards, sniffing furiously at them in the rare chance I'll find our guy.

And that means even more running, no mean feat for a short-legged Corgi like me. Or is that no mean feet, I can't help but ask myself with a chuckle. Oh, for gosh sakes, Moose must be starting to rub off on me. What a truly frightening thought!

Anyway, there's literally no time to spare, so I'm off to work without even thinking about the possible consequences. And I am Ginger, after all, at least as far as anyone out there knows at this very moment, so I figure they'll cut me some slack before anyone thinks to step forward and pull me off the parade grounds.

There's a fine balance between speed and accuracy, and a dog's nose is really no different in the end. Especially when you've been running at top speed and your breath is huffing and puffing out of your chest like an old steam locomotive. And as I race across the gap between the palace and the guards, kicking my two hind legs together in sync like a rabbit, I half expect one of the guards to react, maybe lean down and grab me by the collar or something. But no, these humans have been exceedingly well trained to carry out their planned maneuvers regardless of what random distractions might possibly pop up in the meantime. Like a tourist's camera. Or a red-headed Corgi galloping toward them at full tilt.

And that works perfectly in my favor. As I run down the first line of guards, sniffing each and every one of them as I go past, I can see their eyes following me the entire way, but otherwise not a single one of them so much as twitches a muscle. I make the turn and take on the second line of guardsmen with the same result, and I'm just making my turn for the third and last line when suddenly it hits me. That smell. That unmistakable odor. It's faint, but still—

I hit my brakes at full stride and screech to a halt, pulling up so fast I almost stumble over my front paws. I spin in place, sniffing like my life depends upon it, and there it is again. No question this time. I glance up at the guard's face, but with the steep angle and his chinstrap I just can't be sure.

Part of me remembers what Victoria said about how the smell could be something several of the guards have in common, so I know I need further proof that I've cornered the right man. I can see his eyes now boring straight at me, but so far he hasn't made any move to escape, so I can't be sure.

And then it comes to me. Leaping forward, I shove my well-proportioned Corgi nose up under the left leg of his pants and flip it up. The cuff of his pants only rises a few inches, and even then for barely a split second, but as it turns out that's more than enough for my purposes. Because right there, mere inches from my face, I see it. Bite marks in the leather of his boots. Corgi bite marks, a perfect match for my own deadly choppers. Just like the Canadian Royal Mounted Police, this Corgi has found her man!

But finding him isn't enough. I can tell immediately he knows I've pinned a solid ID on him, and the rigidity that has marked his stature along with all of the other guards is now completely gone, replaced instead by a look of full-on panic. And anger, lots of anger, all of that emotion is apparently directed full-bore at me.

And I have another problem. Even though I'm now one hundred percent sure I've found one of the inside Russian agents involved in Ginger's dognapping, convincing the humans of that rather critical fact is going to take some doing. Particularly since they don't even know Ginger is missing. And particularly since they think they're now staring right down at that very same chief of station.

But just when I begin to think I've found a way to rescue certain defeat from the jaws of victory, I remember the story about how the original Ginger made her mark on the Queen and her palace guards, and I realize it's time to leave my own mark. The fake guard is already preparing to take off running when I jump up on his leg instead and take out a hunk of flesh just above the top of his boot! Well, I didn't actually tear off any flesh, but I sure made certain it sure felt like I did, holding on to his leg with every muscle I have in my muzzle as he kicked and swatted and erupted with a long string of what I feel sure were quite classic and extremely rude Russian obscenities.

This is the part where being mistaken for the real Ginger really paid off. Rather than questioning my attack on one of their own, the other guards close ranks immediately and grab him from behind with both arms. As soon as I'm sure they have him locked up tight I let go of his leg and back off, still snarling, with Victoria and Phineas racing up to flank me protectively. A might late for that, now, but whatever, you know?

The Queen's Guards have now finally come to a full realization that the guy I took a chunk out of is an imposter, and they seem ready to frog march him off for questioning. Suddenly it dawns on me that this Ivan guy that the unmasked guard was talking to might decide to off poor little Ginger and dump her body in the Thames just to hide the most critical evidence of his own involvement in the whole sordid caper. So, with time of the essence, I need to let the guards know how to hunt down Mr. Ivan, and fast. I remember how the fake guard slid his cell phone into his right pocket when he was done talking, and looking over at his legs I can clearly see the unmistakable bulge of his flip phone. Even as out of breath as I am, I lunge forward one last time, grabbing the top of his pocket with my teeth and ripping his pocket wide open from top to bottom. One of the guards, quick-thinking for a human, manages to catch the phone before it even hits the ground.

"Well, what do we have here?" he says, holding the phone up to his face and flipping it open. It only takes him a couple of button presses before he turns and shows the screen to one of his buddies.

"Ivan?" his buddy says, pointing to a long list of phone calls made to just one contact in particular. "I think we may just need to pay a right neighborly visit to this mister Ivan, don't you think, Alfred? A right neighborly visit, indeed!"

Barkingham Palace

N ow that the police are busy trying to track down the Russian spy's friend, Ivan, the immediate challenge for Phineas, Victoria and me is to try and get out in front of them somehow and rescue Ginger before the humans get there. Sure, it's possible the humans could pull off the rescue and free Ginger without a fuss, but really, how often does that happen? Nine times out of ten they let things get out of hand, and someone—or some dog, in this case—winds up getting hurt. Or worse.

Phineas was able to reach Q'ute using some kind of contraption he calls the 'Tellyvator', and her lab rats have managed to hack into the computers at Scotland Yard and grab a copy of the contents off the spy's captured cell phone. Now we're just waiting for them to use the purloined number for Ivan's phone to triangulate his position, and Victoria already has an assault team standing by ready to swoop in ahead of the cops. My job, of course, hasn't really changed all that much, now that we've uncovered the spy operation embedded inside the Queen's Guards—I'm supposed to lay low here at Barkingham, pretending to be Ginger until they can free the real Ginger and get her back to the palace. Which is a role I'm perfectly fine with, especially since my efforts thus far have been amply rewarded with several special treats from the Queen's kitchen!

One thing keeps bothering me, however. While Moose and I have been busy dealing with this secret mission, what happens if Helen gets home and finds the two of us missing? As rough as things have been for her the past few months, and especially all the arguments she's been having with my master Howard, the last thing she needs to worry about is our whereabouts. And worse, if she starts worrying about our chasing off somewhere away from the marina and getting hurt, she may not let us use the doggie door anymore to go outside when she's away running errands. And that would be just terrible, let me assure you. Stuck inside that little boat with Moose running his mouth off all day? I'd go absolutely bonkers.

Just then Myrna the intern wanders by, and I pull her aside to voice my concerns. I'm only halfway through laying it all out for her when she gives me a reassuring wag of her bobbed-off tail and lays a soft paw on my shoulder.

"Oh, you needn't be fretting about all that, Miss Bella," she tells me in her quiet British voice. "Miss Victoria has it all under control. She arranged for stand-ins to take your place just as soon as General Mountbatten collected you this morning. When your mistress gets home she'll find them snoozing away on your yacht, happy as clams they'll be."

I'm not sure why anyone would think clams are all that happy—from what I understand, they're generally yanked up from out of their homes and thrown into steaming cauldrons of hot boiling water before they're summarily dispatched into the maws of hungry humans, but that's neither here nor there, I suppose. The point is, when Helen gets home, she'll expect us both to pop out of our nappies and greet her enthusiastically. Surely she'll notice—

"I know what you're thinking, ma'am," Myrna says, again with that gentle, reassuring tone, "but they'll do just fine. Trust me, your mistress will be so caught up in her own troubles she'll never know the difference."

"But my tail—"

"We found a fake tail extension in a shop in Soho that will do the trick quite nicely, so long as she doesn't get too close, and our two agents have been instructed to minimize that kind of contact at all costs. So you needn't worry—we have everything completely under control. And with Ginger back in the Palace by late afternoon at the latest, you and Agent Moose should be softly ensconced back home on your yacht well before din-din."

Whew! That takes a real load off my shoulders. I mean, I know how the world is supposed to work, that humans are supposed to spend all their time worrying about us, making sure all of our needs are cared for, but still, I can't help thinking about all the burdens Helen is carrying these days on her own slender shoulders. And about how she stepped up at the last minute to save me from a dire and uncertain future at the hands of canine traffickers just a few months back, back in Chicago. That's a favor I'm not sure I can ever fully repay.

Myrna looks like she's just about to leave when a small device attached to her right wrist buzzes. She glances down like she's reading something, then glances back up at me.

"They've got the address for the other spy, mum, and they're closing in as we speak. It'll only be a matter of minutes, now, before we'll know for certain—"

She doesn't have to finish that sentence for me to know exactly what she's thinking. It will only be a matter of minutes before we'll know whether they'll find Ginger safe and sound, or—

Barkingham Palace

giant celebration has broken out throughout the palace as the news comes in. Ginger is safe, and on her way back to Barkingham! The crisis is over!

According to what Myrna's told me, the operation went off without a hitch, with one set of dogs breaking through the front door of the little flat in the East End while other dogs poured in through the windows. In mere seconds the Russian was surrounded by a team of German Shepherd commandos, snarling and snapping and commanding instant respect in a way only that breed can really ever seem to pull off. Ginger was found all trussed up in a back room, understandably upset but otherwise in reasonably good shape. The commandos held their position until the humans finally showed up on the scene, then quickly faded away into the woodwork as the British police burst through the already broken door and took the Russian into captivity.

"Actually, mum, it's unfortunate that we have to leave him to the humans," Myrna tells me, shaking her head. "As wonderful as it is to have Ginger back safe and sound, it would still be nice to know why she was dognapped in the first place. And with the humans now taking charge of the interrogations, it'll likely be many months before we know any of that, if in fact they find out anything at all."

I'll have to agree with her on that. Humans can be so inept when it comes to even the simplest of tasks. Like interrogations. You can good cop bad cop all you want, but there is nothing like a big bad Doberman with a good set of choppers on him to get a guy to spilling the beans fast and furious.

But that's all someone else's problem. With Ginger on her way home now, my job is pretty much done here. I wander over to the kitchen one last time to see if I can snag another treat before the lab rats show up to get this red dye off my fur. And then I guess it's time to head back home to Helen. And Moose.

And I must admit I can't wait to see the look on his face when he finds out I'm the dog who broke this entire case wide open.

Moose

Limehouse Marina

We got the good news about Ginger over my collar phone, and with the dognapping case now closed, there's really nothing left for me to do but head home before Helen gets wise to our little switcheroo and calls the cops to hunt us down.

Dodger was pretty insistent on staying with me all the way back to the boat, but once we caught the Circle Line over to the Tower Hill tube station, I managed to convince him that his time was better spent staying on top of the search for Barkus Johansen and our old Russian friend, especially now that Bella has turned up a Russian mole inside the Queen's own guard.

At the end of the day—quite literally, now—it still doesn't make much sense. Why kidnap Ginger, especially given the fact that, other than obviously the entire English security apparatus, not a single human being had even the foggiest idea of her real role within Barkingham Palace. To the rest of the world, she was just another one of the Queen's pet Corgis, albeit a strikingly different color of Corgi from all of the other pet Pembrokes.

But figuring all that out is way above my kibble grade, and by my own internal clock it is already way past my kibble time, so when I jump off the train at the Limehouse Overground station, I've pretty much got one thing and one thing only on my mind. Din din.

As it turns out, my timing couldn't have been more perfect, because as I start down the steps toward the marina I can see Bella off in the distance, trotting toward the small bridge that leads to our boat.

"Hey, Bella," I bark loudly. And that was unfortunate, because it causes more than a few heads to turn my way. Never a good idea when you're trying to sneak on and off public transportation without some do-gooder human raising a righteous fuss about it all. And, even worse, never a good idea when you're working undercover as an international dog of mystery.

But the bark does serve to stop Bella in her tracks, and she waits up for me as I bounce down the steps and make the turn onto the narrow street that runs along the water beneath the tracks.

"Hey, Moosie," she says coyly when I finally trot up to her. "Did you hear the news?"

I decide to act coy back. No need to let her know that Dodger and I had slept through the whole thing in a dark corner of the Westminster tube station. "You mean about them finding Ginger? And uncovering a nest of Russian spies within the palace? Sure. Glad my little plan worked out."

"*Your* plan? What do you mean, your plan?" And with that she proceeds to share with me every single piddling detail of how she had single-handedly foiled the Russian plot and located the dognapped Ginger tied up in a small apartment, evidently not all that far from here in the East End. And when I say every small piddling detail, I mean even the details about when she had to take a small piddle along the way. You know Corgis—when they start to yakking, it would take an act of Congress to get them to shut up. Or, I guess, since we're in England now, an act of Parliament.

And I can't help but feel a little jealous about it all. I mean, here I am, a Double-O secret agent out on assignment in the field, and here she just kind of stumbles into unmasking the Russian agents. Not

171

exactly the model of modern spycraft, if you know what I mean. More like when you accidentally push a button and somehow wind up blowing up the evil mastermind's secret lair. That sort of thing.

Still, if it had to be anyone other than me that uncovered the plot, I'm glad in a way it was Bella. Other than the fact that I know I'll be hearing about it nonstop—over and over and over—pretty much until the end of time.

Thankfully, the walkie to the boat is fairly short, so she's just on her second recap of the day's events when we pull up alongside. I can see that the front door is open, so apparently Helen's back home. Good. Like I said, it's way past time for din dins! Bella and I carefully make the switch-off with our body doubles on the down low, then swing through the doggie door the moment they're out of sight to do our eager meet-and-greets with our mistress.

Limehouse Marina

W hy, it's about time you two lazy bones noticed I'm home," Helen squeals as Bella tries to knock her flat by jumping on her front legs while I do my usual dance-in-a-circle routine. "I was just about ready to go outside to check on whether you'd both moved on to doggie heaven while I was gone. And, oh, dear me, look at the time! I was so busy at the shop I didn't notice it has gotten so late. You two must be absolutely famished."

That particular comment has me racing for the cupboard where she stores all of our dog food and treats. Just in case she's forgotten where all that is located. Like I've said many times before, humans can be amazingly dense at times. It's amazing they can even find their way home most days.

Luckily, that isn't the problem here, as Helen follows where my nose is pointing and pulls out a large can of the wet stuff. We're in for a real treat tonight! Not quite as tasty as my lunch, for sure, but then food doesn't usually waste much time on my tongue, anyway.

I've just tucked my nose down into my bowl and am busy trying to race Bella to the bottom when Helen's phone rings. Not her cell phone, but an honest-to-God land line, if you can believe it. Helen has always been a little on the old-fashioned side of things.

"Mother! How sweet of you to call. I got home a few minutes ago and saw that you'd rung earlier, and was just feeding the dogs before calling you back…"

If she'd been using the cell phone, I could probably have heard the voice on the other end of the line, but with that land line receiver pressed tightly to her ear, I can only make out a word or two at best. But it's pretty easy to fill in the gaps from what Helen is saying back.

"No, of course I look forward to talking to you, Mother, I just had some errands I needed to run…"

"Well, I can't exactly just sit here waiting for your calls. And you could have tried me on my cell…"

"No, you're right, I shouldn't use that tone with you. And it's so good to hear your voice. Other than the dogs, I'm pretty much all alone out here. Just as I predicted, Howard has been on the road almost nonstop ever since we moved…"

"Yes, I know he has to make a living for us, Mother, but if his job really does require all that traveling, well, then, I could have just stayed behind in Chicago, is all I'm saying. There was no need to sell off almost everything I own and move all the way out here where I don't know a single soul…"

"Yes, yes, of course I've tried to make friends. I try every day. But when you live on a boat in a marina, you don't really have any neighbors to speak of, only folks floating through on their way to someplace else. Or tourists renting out a boat for a week or so before returning home. And it's not like I have all that much in common with any of the other folks in this place…"

"Really? Find work? You don't think I've tried, Mother? Like I've told you a thousand times before, Howard has a visa that lets him work in this country, but I don't. As far as England is concerned, I'm just supposed to sit on my fat bottom out here, cooking and cleaning for my man like it's the 1950's or something. They won't even let me work as a simple store clerk, running a cash register or something like I did in college. And it's not just about the money. I can't even seem to interest anyone in letting me volunteer anywhere. I don't have any children, so the local schools just arch their eyebrows at me suspiciously whenever I ask if I can help out, and for the life of me I haven't found anything even remotely resembling the church we left behind…"

"No, I'm not saying that I'm pushing God out of my life, Mother, just that…"

"Well, it's not really all that easy…"

"Oh, dear, why do I even try?" Helen pulls the phone away from her ear for a second with a long sigh, then shakes her head slowly and puts it back. "Let's change the subject. How's Daddy doing?"

"Oh, I'm so sorry to hear that. What does the doctor say?"

"Well, at least it sounds like he's getting over it. You think he might feel well enough to come visit me out here sometime in the next few months?"

"No, no, of course I understand, Mother. If he's never really ever even left the county, much less the state, how in the world would he ever survive a visit to this strange country? Even if they do sort of speak English. But what about you? I'm sure I can scrape up enough change out of my mad money jar for a round trip ticket…"

"Oh, surely Daddy isn't *that* helpless, Mother. I mean, he can dress himself, and he can always go down to the diner for dinner. It would do him good to get out of the house for a change…"

"Well at least promise me you'll think about it, okay?"

"What? No, I'm sorry, but I don't think I can possibly make it home for Christmas this year. With Howard on the road all the time, I don't have anyone to watch the dogs while I'm gone, and it simply isn't practical to try and fly them both to America and back…"

"Yes, I realize it would be easier if I hadn't taken on the extra dog, but still…"

"I don't know when Howard will be back. We've been over all that already, Mother…"

"That is so not fair, and you know it…"

"Because—because the last time he came home he had perfume on his collar!"

"No, Mother, I'm sure it wasn't my perfume. I don't even wear perfume…"

"No, of course, you're right. If I did pay a little more attention to him, to his *needs*, do things like wearing perfume every now and then, or change the way I dress when he's around, then maybe he wouldn't…"

"Yeah, like that's the way you ever acted around Daddy while I was growing up, flitting around the house like some kind of common tart. Remember, Mother, I was there. No way you were ever going to…"

"No, I'm not saying you mistreated Daddy, just that…"

"Well, I guess that will have to do, Mother. I'm sorry to have put you out like this." She pulls the phone away again for a second with another long sigh. "Look, like I told you earlier, I've been out all day running errands, and the dogs have just eaten and need to find someplace to relieve themselves. Why don't I call you again tomorrow when you're not so upset and we can talk again?"

"No, Mother, I am not putting the dogs' needs above yours. It's just that they've been stuck on this boat all day and they really need to…"

"Look, Mother, I get enough of that kind of nonsense from Howard, and I'm not about to listen to it from you. I am not giving the dogs away, and that's final. They're pretty much all the comfort I have left out here, the only real companions I have left..."

"I understand, Mother, but I can't do anything about that right now. You're not going to be left alone, Daddy will come through this thing just fine, you'll see. He's as strong as an ox."

"And every bit as stubborn as a mule," she tells Bella and me, placing one hand over the receiver for a moment with an impish smile.

"What, Mother? No, I was just telling the dogs to sit. They're getting a bit antsy for their evening constitutional, is all. So I gotta run..."

"I promise, Mother. I'll call you first thing tomorrow morning, your time, okay?"

"Right, well, I love you, too. And give Daddy a big hug from me when he wakes up from his nap..."

"Okay, then. Bye for now!"

She places the receiver on the hook and stands silently in front of it for a long moment, staring at the phone with a hand pressed hard to her forehead. "H-E-double-hockey-sticks!" she mutters, mostly to herself. "Whatever am I going to do with my life? I never should have agreed to come here in the first place!"

Finally, she pulls her hand down and reaches over to where our leashes are hanging from a hook next to the front door.

"Sorry. That wasn't meant for you," she says, wearing a smile that doesn't look entirely convincing. "Mommy's just—tired. But—who really needs a man all that much, anyways? Come on, you guys. Let's go for a walkies."

I don't have to be told twice. Even if I've already put in a week's worth of walkies today.

Limehouse Marina

'm curled up nice and snug in the bed next to Helen as the first orange rays of sunlight start streaking across the morning sky outside. I don't know if I've mentioned it, but living out on the water in London can get pretty cold at night, no matter what time of year it is. And now that summer's pretty much come and gone, I'm usually more than happy staying under the covers until Helen gets up out of bed and starts the fire in the corner. Bella doesn't seem to be as bothered by the cold, though. Probably because she's wearing an extra layer of fat to keep her warm.

Speaking of which, Bella's curled up in her own bed on the floor next to us, snoring away like a runaway locomotive, so I almost don't hear it at first. A small plinking sound, like water dripping in the bathroom. But that sort of thing isn't really my problem, so I dig down deeper into the covers to block out the light.

There it goes again! *Plink. Plink plink.* I poke one eye out to see if I can make out what's causing it. *Plink.* It sounds like it's coming from the porthole on the side of the boat next to the dock, but that doesn't make much sense…

Plink. Okay, I'm clearly not going to get any sleep with all this nonsense going on. I better find out what's causing all this racket and put a stop to it. Crawling out from underneath the covers, I feel an involuntary shiver creep down my backbone. From the cold, I'm pretty sure. Standing up on all fours, I'm still too short to see out the porthole, so I stick my forepaws up on the headboard to get an extra foot or so of height. And right away I can see what's causing the plinking sound. Dodger is standing all by himself out on the dock beside us, tossing small pebbles at our bedroom window.

Limehouse Marina

O bviously, Dodger's not going to go away any time soon unless I go outside and find out what's got him denting up the side of our boat at the crack of dawn this morning like some kind of crack-crazed teenaged vandal. Oh, and did I mention it is really cold right about now? Bone chilling cold. And that's inside the boat.

Helen didn't bother to lock down the doggie door last night, so I drop down off the bed and slip past Bella, still snoring away in her bed. No need to get her all stirred up until I find out what Dodger wants. Once Bella gets riled up she tends to stay riled, and I figure it's probably best to let that sleeping dog lie for now.

I stick my head outside the doggie door, leaving the rest of me inside the boat, where the temperature is at least several degrees warmer than it is outside. Still cold, but hey, every little bit helps.

"Dodger! What the heck?" I call out, trying to keep my voice down so I don't wake up either Bella or my mistress.

Dodger swings around to the front of the boat where he can see me. "Moose! We've got a situation!"

183

A situation? That doesn't sound good, not good at all. Reluctantly I pull the rest of my body through the doggie door, carefully easing it closed so it doesn't slap back and forth noisily behind me. I know in my heart it isn't freezing outside, not yet at least, but still the cold metal deck is sending frosty shivers up through my paws and legs. I stomp down hard to try and shake it off.

"Okay, Dodger, you've got my attention. And ruined what promised to be a nice, well-deserved sleep-in this morning. So, what's going on? Why are you up so early drumming up such a fuss?"

Dodger gives me an irritated look. "Early? Why, I've already been up and about for 'ours!" He glances down the length of our boat with an appraising eye. "Wait a second. I thought you said you guys lived on a yacht. This is no yacht. This is nothing more than a glorified Dutch scow."

"Yeah, well, the yacht's in the shop at the moment," I lie. I'm not sure exactly why I lied, it's not like I have anything to prove here, and I'm not really the person who came up with that bit about living on a yacht in the first place, but still… "Never mind that. Why were you throwing rocks at my bedroom window

184

at a time when even the chickens have the sense not to crawl out of bed?"

Dodger takes one more look at the boat and kind of shrugs. "Whatever," he says, hopping down off the dock onto the deck beside me. "Look, Moose, we got some action overnight on the bug I placed on Barkus Johansen. Just before midnight 'e left the official residence and headed down to Westminster Station, where we were holed up yesterday afternoon. Not too long after that, we lost the GPS signal on the tracker, probably because 'e was too far underground to stay connected to the satellites. But we did get an audio feed of sorts from the bug."

He pulls what looks like a small cell phone out of his pack and pushes a button. Immediately sound starts coming out of a speaker on the front of the device, what sounds like a recording of some sort, a conversation going on between two or maybe three people. I recognize Johansen's voice immediately, but not the second voice, although whoever it is has a pretty strong accent. Russian, I'm going to guess.

Between the funny accents and the poor quality of the recording, full of squeeks and squeals and a steady drone of background noise, it's almost impossible to hear what they're saying. "Dodger, isn't there some way to clean this up? They might as well be talking Chinese for all I know."

"Yes, I'm with you on that. Evidently, the meeting took place somewhere deep underground, so the audio signal is quite spotty. Like I said, we lost the GPS tracker entirely, just after Johansen entered Westminster Underground Station. Q'ute has been working on cleaning it all up, and in fact, this is the best she's been able to accomplish so far." He puts the cell phone thingy away and pulls out his little reader device instead, scrolling down a few pages before looking up again. "From what we can make out, most of the conversation centered around the arrest of the two Russian agents, both quite obviously in the back pocket of Mr. Kitn. And, even more interesting under the circumstances, that was a fact that did not seem to catch Mr. Johansen at all by surprise."

"So he was in on it the entire time?" I ask incredulously.

"Apparently so. They didn't say anything about what their agents were up to, or why they dognapped Ginger, but evidently the arrests have completely bolloxed up their original plans. Leading them to unleash their backup strategy. Johansen called it 'Plan B,' and the best we could make out is, they plan to set off a huge bomb on 'the QE2 line,' or at least that's what we think Kitn called it. The audio sort of comes in and out at that point."

"The cutey two line? What the heck's that?" I ask.

"M thinks it's a reference to the Cunard Line, a cruise ship company that originally owned and operated the cruise ship Queen Elizabeth 2. That boat was decommissioned in 2008 and is now functioning as an 'otel down in Dubai."

"So Kitn plans to set off a bomb in Dubai? Then why is he here in London, and what possible connection is there between Johansen and Dubai?"

"Like I said, Moose, M thinks the target is not the QE2, but instead Cunard, a British–American cruise line based at Carnival 'ouse in Southampton, on the southernmost tip of England. Cunard still operates the QE2's sister ship, the Queen Mary 2, an ocean liner that by no small coincidence is scheduled to dock at Southampton sometime tomorrow morning. And that ties in perfectly with another comment Kitn made toward the end of the conversation, that the overall objective of Plan B is to 'blow up the Queen.' And if they do manage to pull that off, especially while the ship is still at sea, that could spell the deaths of almost 4,000 passengers and crew. A terrorist attack of unspeakable dimensions. And it's even worse. The Queen Mary 2 has a special section of the ship devoted to the luxurious transportation of dogs and cats across the ocean from New York to Southampton. It's one of the few alternatives to shipping pets overseas in the cargo 'old of jet airliners. If that bomb does go off, there's no way the humans are going to make any kind of effort to get them into the lifeboats. Every single one of those pets will wind up going down with the ship. Down to the very bottom of the ocean, drowned in their crates with no 'ope of survival."

Whoa! Now that I think back on it, Helen and Howard had a long argument about sending Bella and I to England on a cruise ship. That must have been the same one! In fact, we could very well have been onboard that boat at this very moment, happily finishing off our breakfasts, blissfully unaware of the mortal danger that lay just beneath our paws. I wipe a bead of sweat off my forehead.

"But where does that leave us, Dodger? I mean, I assume the humans have already dispatched a team to the ship to locate and disarm the bomb. So why the visit from you this morning? What could Bella and I possibly do to help stop Kitn and Johansen from carrying out their diabolical plans?"

Dodger checks the doggie door again, but evidently Bella is still dead asleep inside. He leans in closer. "M thinks it's imperative that we capture Kitn and Johansen ASAP, just in case we can't locate the bomb in time. And of course, we 'ave no idea when exactly they plan to set it off. As far as we know, they may also have a remote control hooked up to it, and if they find out we're on to them…"

I nod, finishing off the thought. "They'll set it off early, while the ship is still way out at sea, and everyone will die."

"Exactly. So you and I are reactivated, Double-O-Ten. Johansen 'asn't returned to his residence at Downing Street, and his GPS tracker is still not pinging. So we don't 'ave a lot to go on, I'm afraid, but we'll just' 'ave to make do with what we've got."

"Gotcha. And I suppose you've got those stand-in dogs ready to fill in for Bella and I while we're off on the mission."

"Stand-in dog, Moose. As in just one dog. For you. Bella's not needed at the palace anymore, now that Ginger's back. So she'll be staying behind on the boat. That'll work out better as a cover for you, anyway, letting the doppelganger pretend to sleep while she keeps your mistress preoccupied."

"Gotcha. Okay, give me a sec to touch base with Bella and let her in on the plan, then I'm good to go. You said we don't have much in the way of leads. So where do we head first?"

"There's a man who lives deep in the Chinatown district of London who M says always 'as one ear to the ground when it comes to bombs, so we can start there."

Now I can see where my expertise really comes into play in all of this. "Ooh, yeah, I saw that trick once, back during the Southside Prison break. We were trying to figure out exactly where to place the bomb, so one of us went up on top to make a lot of noise while Pappy pressed his ear…"

Dodger looks momentarily confused, but then it clears. "No, Moose, what I meant was, 'he's pretty well connected with all of the bombmakers and the guys peddling timers and remotes in this town. So if the bomb originated in London, he's sure to 'ave a bead on who built it."

"Uh, yeah, that's what I meant." I look back at the doggie door. "And—uh—by the way, not wanting to be a problem or anything, but you got here kinda early this morning, before Helen could set out my breakfast. Any way we could wait until—"

"No time for that, Moose. The clock is literally ticking away on us as we speak. But I brought a few 'igh-protein doggie biscuits in my pack that should 'old us until we can get a chance to grab something more substantial."

"W-e-l-l, okay," I finally agree, given that I apparently have few alternatives, and the even more important fact that quite a few dog and cat lives are at stake here. But the mere mention of the word 'stake' makes me think of 'steak,' and my mouth is already starting to water. "Any way one of those is bacon? 'Cause I love bacon. And it is breakfast, after all."

It takes me less than a minute to wake up Bella and give her the news, and Dodger has the bacon bar unwrapped and ready for me as I jump up off the prow of the boat onto the dock. It's already half gone by the time we make the short bridge over the canal that leads out into the Thames, on our way to Chinatown. Wherever that might be.

Chinatown

O nce again we decide to take the underground. I'll have to say, it's all pretty convenient, almost as easy as the elevated trains back in Chicago, although there's like a bazillion steps to navigate to get down to the underground trains, and by the time we're on our way my little legs are almost exhausted.

We get off at Piccadilly Circus Station, and when we finally emerge from the station I'm feeling pretty much confused.

"Say, Dodger, where the heck is the circus?" I ask, looking around and seeing nothing but the usual London traffic and shops.

"Say what?" Dodger asks, pulling up short.

"Circus. Where is the Piccadilly circus?"

"Oh, that." Dodger smiles at me, a funny kind of smile I'm getting a lot lately. "Well, Moose, the word 'circus' here refers to a roundabout, not some type of theater."

"A roundabout? What's that?" Now I'm even more confused.

"A roundabout is a type of traffic circle, a way for the auto traffic to get through the intersection without having to bother with traffic lights and such." Dodger glances around, now looking almost as confused as I am. "But it appears the circle is missing now. Odd. They must have removed it at some point, but never bothered to change the name of the place. Names have an 'abit of sticking around, you know, especially 'ere in England."

"Oh. I see. No circus, then." It's too bad, really. I was kind of looking forward to taking in a few shows. I mean, who doesn't like a good elephant show every now and then. Except the elephants, of course. I imagine they'd be much happier back where they came from.

Dodger has taken off again, and I am hot on his heels. That is, if he had any heels, being a dog and all. Before long we come into an area of the city that looks a wee bit different. The street signs have changed, and now they have some strange stick figures painted on them right next to the normal lettering. And many of the stores around here don't have normal signs at all, just more of those stick figures, like something out of a crazy pick-up-sticks game. We pass a giant stone statue of what sorta looks like a lion who really needs to go on a diet, and then I hear strange noises up ahead, music of a sort I haven't ever heard before.

"What's going on?" I ask, ducking in and out of the crowded sea of legs, trying to keep up.

Dodger answers over his shoulder, not bothering to look back. If he did, moving as fast as we are right now, I'm pretty sure he'd wind up plowing right into the backside of someone. "Not sure, Moose. I think it may be a parade. They have them every now and then around here. Maybe today is some kind of Chinese holiday."

Just then the crowd seems to part, everyone moving further away from the middle of the street, and suddenly I'm looking straight on at this giant dragon, all red and yellow and taking up most of the street! No wonder everyone's running for their lives! Searing blasts of fire and smoke are billowing out of its mouth, and bright green streamers are wafting behind its head in the breeze, trailing along almost halfway down its back. And did I mention its mouthful of massive, razor sharp teeth, every one of which is easily twice the size of me?

"Holy smokes!" I holler, ducking behind some random human for protection before I end up as a morning snack for the dragon. "Dodger, take cover!"

But when I peek around the leg I'm using for shelter, Dodger doesn't look at all concerned about the mortal danger he's in. Instead he's just standing there, laughing, as the dragon bears down straight at us, roaring so loud it's making my molars shake. Not to mention what it's doing to my tummy.

"Ha ha! Moose, you're a regular comedian," he says, now stepping out of the way of the dragon and continuing down the street, like he could care less that there's a hundred ton lizard pounding along the street just a few feet off to his side. I don't know how he does it, but I push further into the crush of human legs and eventually work my way past the dragon as well. That dog must have ice water in his veins is all I can figure. And that would be pretty handy right now, given all the fire and smoke that dragon is flinging around like it's the annual meeting of Flamethrowers Anonymous.

Anyway, in just a few soul shattering minutes the dragon has somehow completely disappeared behind us, and we're slipping past some kind of all-Chinese band that's following along right behind it, clearly warning everyone of what's coming at them down the street, when without any warning Dodger sticks out a paw and darts through the middle of the band into a dark, narrow alley. It's all I can do to keep up with him without getting trampled underfoot or beaten with a drumstick, but I somehow make it across the street in one piece and find him standing in front of what appears to be a run-down liquor store, eyeing it up and down.

Dodger points toward the doorway. "The bloke we're looking for runs this little offie," he tells me, like I have any idea what offie means. Dodger's found a tight crack in the wall beside the offie, though, and is squeezing through. "It's a bit of a tight fit, mate, but I think we can make it a'right."

I have to adjust my blue collar and suck in my gut a little, but soon we're through the crack and standing at the rear of the building. A dark and menacing doorway leads inside.

"Follow me," Dodger says, turning the knob on the door and pushing it open. Like that's not what I've been doing pretty much nonstop since we left the marina this morning. Fighting against my better judgment, I climb the steps and join him inside.

197

It takes a few moments for my eyes to adjust to the darkness, but after a bit I can see a long hallway stretching out in front of us. There are doors spaced about ten feet apart on either side of the hall, all closed and presumably locked. I watch each one of them carefully as we slide past, wary that some Jack the Ripper type might jump out at any moment to cut us to pieces. Or worse.

After what seems like a lifetime we're finally past the doors and emerge into the back of the front of the liquor store. The light here is a little better, what little bit of light that has managed to snake its way down the alley and then in through the grimy windows at the front of the store. Instinctively I turn my head to check out the shadowy area off to my right. Nothing. Then I turn left, and find myself staring face-to-face with the business end of the biggest, blackest gun I've ever seen.

Chinatown

The owner of the gun is an old, withered-looking Chinese dog. A Shar Pei, judging by the Grand Canyon-like folds in his skin, and his black muzzle is pulled back hard in an evil sneer, exposing several sharp, yellowed teeth. He's swinging the gun ever so slowly back and forth between Dodger and me, keeping us both covered while he pulls back the hammer, cocking it, ready to fire.

"Whoa, whoa, 'old on there, Ling Lau," Dodger says, holding up both paws in a placating gesture, a move I quickly mimic. "We don't mean you any 'arm, we just came to ask you some questions."

Ling Lau sights down the barrel of the gun at the center of my forehead, and I'm pretty certain I'm about to wet myself at any moment. "Old Chinese proverb say, dead men ask no questions," he growls with a thick Chinese accent. "I start with this one, then I ask you questions instead."

By "start" I take it to mean he plans to shoot me, and I've got to think of something pretty quick before he manages to pull that trigger and turn me into a dead dog walking. Or not walking, actually. Just lying in a pool of my own blood on the floor.

"Uh, Mr. Lau, you probably don't want to do that, sir. Shoot me, I mean. I'm, uh, kind of a PETSEC Double-O agent, and a hero at that, and, uh, if you shoot me this place will be swarming with agents in minutes. That can't be good for business."

Lau eyes me through tightly slitted eyes, one of which is still trained down the barrel of his gun at my head. "Double-O? You not look like much of a Double-O to me. Matter of fact, you look like scared little purse doggie to me."

Dodger takes that as an invitation to clear his throat, bringing the gun barrel swinging back around to point at his head, instead. I quickly check down by my feet and see that no, I'm still completely high and dry down there. For now.

Dodger somehow forces a disarming smile to appear on his face. Although Mr. Lau is still managing to remain fully armed. "Uh, actually, Mr. Lau, Moose 'ere is correct. He's a Double-O agent, for real. Licensed to kill and all that. But not that we're 'ere to kill anyone," he adds quickly as the gun swings back around in my direction. "Like I said, we just ''ve a few questions to ask, is all. Then we'll leave, and leave you to your business."

Ling Lau seems to be thinking through the whole complicated situation, which I take as a good sign. He leans forward slightly, his gun getting ever so much closer to my head. "Why you two sneak around in back, instead of coming through front door if you just want to ask question?" he snarls.

Dodger has his smile back at full wattage. "Well, now, that wouldn't really do, would it, two PETSEC agents, waltzing in 'ere in full view of everyone 'iding out there in the alley? What would they think? The way I see it, some of those alleyway denizens out there might come to think of you as some kind of stoolie, some kind of rat. Instead of the fine Shar Pei canine that you are."

Ling Lau is shaking his head, slowly, and just as slowly lowers the gun a notch. Now it's just pointing at my chest. "Yes, flowery words. But old proverb say, prettiest flowers grow from soil rich in manure." But despite all that he finally seems to come to some kind of decision and lowers the gun entirely, setting it in his lap. "Okay, then, ask your questions. But warning—

Ling Lau has many very hungry dogs in alley to rip flesh from bones if I just bark. So make it quick."

Dodger lowers his paws, gripping them in front of him and bowing slightly in Ling Lau's direction. "Thank you, honored sir," he says, kneeling down and motioning for me to do the same. "I'll be brief. A Russian agent by the name of Vladimir Kitn has been seen around London over the past few days—"

"I know all about Kitn," Ling Lau snaps back.

"Yes, yes, I'm sure you do," Dodger answers in a soft, respectful tone. "But the thing is, 'e's been implicated in some kind of plot involving Barkingham Palace, and now we've got highly reliable intelligence that tells us 'e's plotting with the PM, Barkus Johansen, to blow up the ocean liner Queen Mary 2. Killing almost four thousand humans and countless numbers of dogs and cats in the process."

"The humans we can do without," Ling Lau suggests. "But the animal loss would be most unfortunate."

"Yes, yes, you're right. And that's precisely why we're here. We think Kitn and Johansen have rigged a massive bomb on board the ship, and plan to trigger it using either a timer device or some type of remote control—"

"And you think I know something of this bomb," Ling Lau says, his eyes tightening again.

"Well, not directly, of course, you would never dirty your paws with something like that," Dodger says quickly. "But indirectly, if that bomb was manufactured 'ere in London, we were 'oping you might have some inkling of where it was made, or who the bomb maker might be."

Ling Lau nods once, then his eyes take on a faraway look, like there's something standing in front of him that only he can see. "Hmm. If I do know something, what is in it for me? As old proverb say, giving away something for nothing sure way for trader to go to bed hungry in the night."

Dodger is looking my way and nodding vigorously. "Of course, of course. I—I don't have anything specific to trade you for that information at the moment, but I can promise you that any 'elp you can give your Queen and country at the moment will not be forgotten—"

"Queen and country. Pah!" Ling Lau spits that out like the words are a foul taste in his mouth. "Ling

Lau have no love for either. But point is made, I trade you favor now for return favor at later time. We have deal?"

Dodger looks to me for confirmation, since technically I'm the senior agent here, even if he has been doing all the talking, and I give him a quick nod yes.

"You've got a deal," Dodger says, now rising back to all fours. I stand up now as well, both of us staring at Ling Lau, who seems to be lost in thought, his eyes studying a far corner of the room. Finally he looks up at me, studying me just as intently. "You quiet one, and he the loud mouth, but you obviously the big boss here," he murmurs. I nod back ever so slightly.

"Very well," he says after a long moment. "A bomb that big, it could only be built in one place, small cottage near the Old Royal Naval College." He stops and grabs a piece of paper off a table at his elbow, scribbling something down on it and passing the paper over to Dodger. "Here is address. But—two more conditions," he adds, still holding tightly to the paper.

"Okay," I agree with no small amount of hesitation.

"First, you not get address from me. My name never mentioned, never even written down in official report."

"Sounds fair," I promise. "What's your second condition?"

"Ha-ha! You get me autographed picture of Daniel Craig," he says, finally breaking into a toothy yellow grin. "He *real* Double-O agent. *Real* James Bond. Not like scrawny little purse doggie."

"I think we can manage that," I say, ignoring the insult for now. Because at least now we have a lead in the case. And an autographed picture is a small price to pay for that, even if I do have to swallow a little pride in the process. After all, a secret agent can't exactly afford to wear his feelings on his sleeve for all the world to see, now can he? Especially since I'm not exactly wearing any sleeves at the moment. Or at any moment, for that matter. I'm not exactly one of those dogs that would be caught dead wearing some stupid purse doggie outfit. And thankfully Helen has the good sense to not even try that kind of thing with me. Especially after the look I gave her when she tried it the first time. And the teeth. Don't forget about the teeth.

Chinatown

We manage to make it out of the alley without further incident, and I immediately race for the first light post I see to relieve some of the pressure that built up while I had that gun pointed at my face.

Dodger wags his eyebrows in my direction. "Wow. Didn't see that coming," he laughs.

"Yeah, well, if we're going to get moving on this, it never hurts to lighten the load when you can."

"Right. I see," he answers, staring down at the small pond I've created. "And by the looks of things, that was quite the load, indeed."

I decide to ignore him and his snarky comments and get back to focusing on the business at hand. Instead of the business trickling down the side of the light pole. "By the way, Dodger, where are we headed now?"

"Greenwich," he says simply.

That really surprises me. "The Grinch? Are you telling me the bomb is located in Whoville? And hey, I always thought that was just a made-up story for all the little pups. But I guess you learn something new every day."

Dodger shakes his head at me with a scowl. "Not the Grinch, Moose. Greenwich. G-R-E-E-N-W-I-C-H. Greenwich."

It takes me a second to work through the spelling. "Oh, you mean Green Witch, like that evil witch in the Wizard of Oz?"

Dodger looks a bit put out again, and for the life of me I can't figure why. "No, Moose, the name is pronounced Greenwich. The W is silent."

Now that makes absolutely no sense, and I don't hesitate to tell him so. "Okay, smarty pants, then explain this to me. Do you call a slab of meat between two slices of bread a Sandich? Or for that matter, are you actually a Norch terrier, instead of a Nor*wich*? Is that how it works?"

"No, it's called a sandwich, you do pronounce the W with that one, but yes, you do drop the W in Norwich. And, by the way, you Americans do the same thing. Pronouncing Arkansas one way and Kansas another, for example."

"Okay, so help me understand this, then. You Brits call something a circus, even though it's not any kind of show at all, then you say a street is a roundabout, when there's nothing round about it in the slightest, and now you're going and dropping perfectly good letters out of the middle of words? Didn't they ever bother to teach you anything about definitions and proper pronunciation here in England? Why, you English dogs are almost as bad as the humans, talking all the time the way they do like they've got a load of marbles bouncing around in their mouths!"

Dodger looks like he's about to say something, then closes his mouth and looks down at his watch. "Look, Moose, we don't 'ave time for any of this... nonsense. We've got a bomb to stop, for flip's sake, and we're quickly running out of time to do so. In fact, I'd suggest we try and call up an Uber instead of futzing around with the Underground or the bus lines."

"An Uber?" I ask him, patting my nonexistent pockets. "And just how are we gonna pay for that? I seem to have left all of my credit cards behind back on the boat."

"You don't need credit cards, Moose. Just use the blue collar. We tell them what we need, and they 'andle all the payments on their end. Charge it to M's account, they do."

Wow. That's a sweet deal for sure. "Well, okay, now we're talking—and hey, notice how I pronounced the L and the K on that one!" I can't help but get one last dig in as I reach up and tap the side of my collar. "Blue collar workers, this is Agent Double-O-Ten. Dodger and I need a ride to—" I motion to Dodger, who shows me the slip of paper we got from Ling Lao, and I quickly recite the address to the folks on the other end.

"Rodger, Ten, we'll have an Uber to you in 60 seconds. Stand by."

I look around quickly to see what it is they want me to stand by, but I don't see anything that really stands out all that much, and since Dodger doesn't seem to be standing by anything in particular I decide to just ignore that comment and stand where I am. And just like the collar said, in almost exactly one minute a smallish cherry red convertible squeals to a stop right in front of us, its chrome wheels and trim gleaming brightly in the midday sun. I glance up and am astonished to see a familiar face behind the wheel.

"Sweet Chocolate!" Dodger squeals beside me. "And my goodness, Trini, what a sweet ride! What is this, a Triumph?"

Trini smiles at us, waving a large hand around flamboyantly. "Why, yes it is, Dodger. A '76 Triumph Spitfire 1500, to be exact. Hop on in, guys!"

"Uh, we're kind of waiting for an Uber," I explain, not wanting to be impolite.

Trini flashes us a broad grin. "Yes indeedy, and as it turns out, I'm your ride! So like I said, hop in beside me. Traffic is light, so I should have you up to Greenwich in well under an hour, or my name isn't Sweet Chocolate."

Trini pronounces the word Greenwich with a silent W, just like Dodger did, so I'm beginning to think I might have been a bit out of line with all of that, but still, I have to go back to what I said about how you pronounce the word "sandwich." And Dodger's breed, the Norwich terriers. The letters are put there for a reason, you know, and when you start tossing them about all willy-nilly like this, well, if you think autocorrect is a problem…

Anyway, once we're both inside the car, the two of us sharing the single passenger seat, Trini takes off like a rocket. He's darting in and out of traffic like a regular Mario Andretti—I think that's the name of that Mario fellow in the video games—and I'm starting to get a little bit jealous of the fact that we canines can't drive. It all seems like tons of fun, but of course the humans have maintained a monopoly on all the licenses. Like so much else in life.

I'm also starting to wonder how Trini knew we needed a ride. "So, Trini," I ask, getting his attention, "do we need to do something to let the Uber driver know we're catching a ride with you instead?"

"Oh, no, little buddy, that won't be necessary. Because I'm the driver they assigned to pick you up in the first place. Well, actually, I was already in the general area when I caught the ride request coming over the wire. Two small terriers, one wearing a bright blue metallic collar, it said. There can't possibly be another dynamic duo matching that particular description anywhere in the city, now can there? So I punched in right away to get the assignment—and there wasn't exactly any real competition for the fare, since picking up random dogs off the street isn't exactly routine for us drivers—and lo and behold, here we are!"

"But I thought you worked for the double-decker buses," Dodger says, gripping the door of the car tightly with one paw as Trini executes a particularly abrupt turn and guns it down a mostly deserted street.

Trini gives us that brilliant white smile of his again. "I do, Dodge, but London is an expensive city, and I can't really make enough money to live here if I'm just punching tickets for tourists—not and have enough money left over to entertain my lady friends, at least—so I started this gig a few months back. Keeps me in the black at the bank, and I get to meet a whole new assortment of interesting people to boot."

I'm not all that sure why he needs money to stay black, and what in the world a bank would have to do with that, anyway, but I hold my tongue for the moment. Like I said earlier, there's a lot about this world I still don't understand. But I'm catching up quick.

Greenwich

We cross the Thames going south, taking an absolutely ginormous bridge right in front of the Tower of London, then turning hard left onto a broad and lightly traveled road. In what seems like no time Trini pulls over to the side of the road just past a huge and quite obviously ancient boat housed in this really humongous glass building, then reaches across the gap to open our door.

"The actual address you're looking for is still about a block or so away," he says, pointing off to our right, "but I figured you wouldn't want to be dropped off in front of it. Especially not in a bright red sports car like this one. A little hard to sneak up on them that way."

I nod my head before following Dodger out the door and into the street. "Yeah, good thinking, Trini." At this rate, I figure we might make a decent spy out of this guy yet.

"Uh, you guys need me to hang around awhile for the return trip?" Trini asks, pointing to a small parking area nearby.

"No, thanks mate, but I think we'll 'ave to leg it from here," Dodger tells him, pushing the car door closed with the flick of a paw. "My guess is we'll be on foot for a while, trying to track down the bomb maker. But, just in case, is there any way to contact you if we change our minds?"

"Sure," Trini tells us with a smile. "I can set up a search protocol on the Uber site for any dogs looking for rides, and that'll notify me right away. But be sure to add in that one of you is wearing a blue collar. That activates certain security protocols that blocks out the unregistered drivers. The ones who aren't exactly read in to the specifics of the whole PETSEC arrangement."

"Will do," Dodger says over his shoulder as he quickly trots toward the corner. I flash Trini a smile of my own as I take off once again in hot pursuit.

It only takes us only a few minutes to reach the cottage, a building that looks to me more like a rundown shack, set back behind an unkempt overgrowth of bushes and small trees. But I suppose that helps to hide whatever nefarious activities the owners are up to inside. Like making bombs to blow up giant cruise ships.

Dodger motions for us to slip around to the back, so I duck under a tree branch and follow him, watching carefully the whole time for anyone spying on us through the windows. But every window we pass is covered tightly in tin foil, so it looks like we're safe for the moment.

At the rear of the house is a small yard, mostly just cracked brown dirt, like nobody has watered it in years. The entire yard is covered in trash, some of it piled up almost halfway up the six-foot wooden fence that surrounds the lot. At the back of the shack is a single door, now hanging ominously open, like someone left in such a rush they didn't bother to close it behind them.

I give Dodger a questioning eye, and he leans over to whisper in my ear. "Ask the collar if they can run an infrared sweep of the place to see if anyone's still 'iding inside. That would be nice to know before we step up into that doorway and make ourselves an easy target for some shooter."

That sounds like a great idea, and I pass the suggestion on to the collar. A voice comes back immediately. "Give us a minute, and we'll run a pass overhead to check it out."

In way less than a minute I hear a noise overhead, and a plain black helicopter shoots across the sky above us, low enough to make it out but still high enough not to make it obvious what they're doing. As soon as it's gone, the collar voice returns. "Infrared says the place is all clear, but I'd still be careful if I were you. They may have set some traps for any unwary intruders."

I nod, even though the collar people can't possibly see me. "Good idea. Thanks."

Dodger motions that he's going to take the lead, and we slip closer to the door, pressing against the back of the house the entire way to stay as invisible to anyone still hiding inside as we can. When we get to the door, Dodger holds up a paw to stop me, then mouths that he'll go in first and that I should wait for his all-clear signal before following.

Slowly he creeps up the steps, keeping his head low until the last possible moment when he pokes it up above the last step, squinting into the darkness beyond. After taking a long look inside—and I can't possibly believe he's seeing much of anything, given how bright it is outside and how dark the unlit interior of the shack is right now—he steps carefully up to the open door, pulling out a light from his little pack and shining it on the floor just inside the door sill, then raising it slightly to get a better view of the room. Apparently satisfied that everything looks safe, he motions for me to join him and steps inside.

When I get through the door, pausing for a few moments to let my eyes adjust to the darkness, it looks to me like someone set off a bomb in the room. Which, considering they actually were building bombs in the place, could quite possibly have happened.

"What the heck happened here?" I ask Dodger in a whispering voice.

"I'm not sure," he answers. "But judging by 'ow they kept up the outside, this may just be the natural state of things. Although you'd think that anyone building a bomb might want to be a bit more— fastidious, wouldn't you say?"

"Actually, I wouldn't think they'd move very fast at all," I tell him. "If I were making a bomb, I'd be sure to take every single step along the way very slowly." While Dodger pokes his head into the other rooms of the house, I check out the shelves lining the small kitchen area, all helter-skelter with wires and alarm clocks and small sticks of what look very much like firecrackers, along with tons of empty boxes labeled C-4, whatever that is. When Dodger gets back, I point out the boxes.

"What are those, Dodge? Are they batteries of some sort? I remember seeing a bunch of C batteries in Helen's junk drawer back in Chicago, and…"

"No, Moose, C-4 is an explosive, one of the most powerful non-nuclear explosives known to dogkind. It's pretty much the go-to explosive agent for bomb makers, because it's also fairly stable until it's detonated. And unlike TNT or the other C compounds, it isn't all that sensitive to temperature changes." He stops talking for a second and swings a paw toward the empty doorway behind him. "Looks like we're too late, the house is completely emptied out. Well, other than all this," he adds, pointing out the junk on the shelves all around us.

"So we've come up empty again?" I ask, all too conscious of the fact that Johansen and Kitn have apparently slipped through our paws once again.

"Well, maybe not entirely," Dodger says, pulling out another small box from his pack, and making me wonder for a moment just how many gizmos he has stuffed inside that tiny little satchel.

He holds it up, pointing with his left paw at the screen. "If C-4 is marked with a taggant agent, such as DMNB, it's possible we can track it with an explosive vapor detector. Hopefully well before it gets detonated." He pushes a button, and the screen lights up. He watches it carefully for a few seconds, then looks up. "I think we may be in luck, Moose. I'm getting a strong reading on the taggant, meaning the bomb was 'ere in this very room until quite recently."

"So we just missed it?" I ask, deflated.

Dodger nods at me with a small smile. "Yes, unfortunately, but with a signal this strong, there's a good chance we can follow its trail if we move quickly."

"What are we waiting for, then?" I stop and point toward the front of the house. "And since the joint is empty, we might as well take the front door."

"Righto. Except that it's clear the bomb went out the back, so the signal will be much stronger if we follow that route." He stops, then leans in toward my collar. "Uh, there's still a lot of explosive material in 'ere, so you blokes might want to send along the bomb squad. And alert Scotland Yard as well. I'm sure they'll find plenty around 'ere to keep them busy for a very long time."

"We're already on it," says the voice in the collar as Dodger starts waving his little bomb detector thingy in the air near the back door.

"This way," he says, not even bothering to look back as his detector starts going bonkers, emitting a loud pinging sound that echoes off the walls of the mostly empty kitchen. Dodger moves quickly to turn down the sound, then steps out through the open back door. "Come on, Moose. We 'ave a bomb to catch, and given the amplitude of the signal I'm getting right now, they can't have gone very far."

I gotta agree. Given the sound Dodger's little do-hickey was putting out, that signal's attitude was just about as bad as they come.

Greenwich

odger's detector thingy has us wandering down the street like a bunch of teenagers staring down at their smartphones, completely oblivious to anything and everything going on around them, and after several near misses with cars, bicycles and pedestrians, we pass the giant glassed-in boat and find ourselves standing in front of what looks like a red brick greenhouse with an all-glass roof and two open doorways on either side of us. The Thames is just a short distance behind it.

Dodger looks momentarily confused. "Huh. I rather thought they'd have used a lorry or something, rather than try and carry the thing into the city on foot." He looks back at me, one eyebrow arched. "Well, Moose, I guess that's why we get the danger pay, what? Time to 'itch up our braces and get on with it, I suppose."

With that he heads for the right-side doorway and down a short spiral stairway, and I can't help but notice a small sign at the entrance.

"Hey, Dodger, this sign says this place is private property, not for public usage."

"Yes, well, we can't always be bothering with signs, now can we?" he answers, plowing ahead down the stairs. I just shrug and follow. He is my native guide, after all.

At the bottom of the stairs we come across a set of doors. Dodger pushes them open and heads into a large tunnel that curves down fairly sharply in the general direction of the river. A few pedestrians and some guy pushing a bicycle pass us and nobody steps up to ask for tickets or anything, so I have to assume Dodger's right about the sign.

As we head deeper into the tunnel, I'm starting to detect a signal of my own, some kind of deep drumming sound coming from the tunnel ahead. A familiar sound, kind of like—

"Dodger! It's the dragon! It's followed us here!" My eyes leap in every direction, and suddenly I spot a small alcove cut into the tiled walls on either side of us. I dive toward the alcove, pulling myself into a fetal position and covering my head with my paws, tail tucked in to my hind end just as tightly as I can manage. The sound has now blossomed into a roar in the short time it takes me to reach a position of relative safety, the sound becoming deafening as it bounces off the ever-present white glazed tiles. In my mind's eye I can already see the blasts of red-hot fire shooting down the tunnel from its mouth, ready to consume anything and everything in its wake. Between my spread toes I see Dodger, still walking forward, acting all nonchalant, careless of the coming danger, and I have a brief thought that the sound may have somehow blasted out his eardrums. He's way ahead of me now, peering down the tunnel, and then he turns back my way, pointing and laughing.

"Moose, you ninny, it's just a gaggle of schoolchildren out on a field trip to the Royal Observatory," he says, laughing, and sure enough, in seconds a sea of young human children appear, all dressed in almost identical outfits, an adult with a small yellow flag waving gaily above her head leading the way. The kids are making an extraordinary amount of noise, dancing about, poking each other, shouting, laughing, singing, and in general making a complete public spectacle of themselves. Not to mention a public nuisance. I'd almost prefer the dragon.

I unwind myself with as much dignity as I can manage, all the while keeping a sharp eye on the mob in front of me and still refusing to dismiss the possibility that a full-fledged dragon could make an appearance inside the tunnel at any moment. Meanwhile, Dodger has stopped laughing, at least audibly, but his eyes betray what he's really thinking.

"Okay, I get it," I admit, "but hey, as I see it, it's just trading one mortal danger for another."

"Whatever," Dodger responds, frowning again, and I get the feeling he would have said more, but he's got that detector thing out again and I can hear the pinging sound even over the ruckus from all the yard apes that are swarming past us like we're Noah parting the Red Sea with a pillar of salt or something.

The rest of the way down the tunnel is mostly uneventful, folks meandering along, minding their own business for the most part. Finally the tunnel starts curving up, and in minutes we emerge from the tunnel through a domed structure almost identical to the one we entered on the other side. There's a short flagpole outside with a green flag I don't recognize, and a small brick building that calls itself the "Island Gardens Café," but otherwise no sign of any bomb. We make our way past a set of yellow-brick apartments, then past a fire station, and eventually end up outside a nondescript dirty white warehouse.

Dodger is waving his detector thing around in the air furiously. "It's gone!" he says, frowning again. "The signal is gone!"

"Do you think they accidentally set off the bomb?" I ask, checking all around for blast damage.

Dodger shakes his head as he twists a knob on the front of the detector. "No, as big as that thing 'as to be to damage a ship as large as the Queen Mary 2, we'd 'ave heard it all across London. Heck, we'd 'ave 'eard it 'alfway across England, for that matter. So it was 'ere, then it was not. That can mean only one thing. They must 'ave loaded it up on a lorry and hauled it away."

"Then we've lost them. And lost the bomb. Now we'll never find it," I suggest, suddenly feeling a little dispirited. We were so close!

"Maybe not," Dodger tells me, pointing up into the sky. I follow his paw and see a small camera mounted inconspicuously up on an electrical pole. "We 'ave cameras situated all across the city, so with any luck we can look back at the recordings and figure out where they took the bomb, and when." He stops, rubbing his muzzle for a second. "It's awful strange, though, when you think about it."

"What's strange?" I ask, noticing for the very first time just how many cameras were stationed way up in the sky, looking down on pretty much everything that ever happens in London. I get an involuntary shiver down my back just thinking about it. Don't these English people understand the concept of privacy?

Dodger is speaking again, interrupting my thoughts. "Well, the readings I've been getting are all relatively fresh, but if the bomb is actually intended for the Queen Mary like we suspect, they're cutting their timelines pretty tight. I mean, we just assumed that the bomb was loaded on the ship back in New York City. Now, with the bomb just now being loaded onto the lorry, they'd 'ave to move it onboard the ship in the middle of the bloody ocean, and it baffles me how they could ever manage to pull that off. Particularly since they now 'ave almost no time to spare before the boat makes harbor at Southampton."

"Maybe they have a submarine or something," I suggest.

"Yes, well, still there's the problem of timing. A submarine is incredibly slow…"

"They could fly the bomb out to sea in a float plane, then meet up with the submarine just before the cruise ship gets there!" I add, and as soon as I say it I'm pretty much convinced that's exactly how they'll try to pull it off. It's how I would do it, after all.

"Hmm. Possibly." Dodger stares off down the road for a second, then stashes his detector gadget in his pack and turns my way. "Blue collar, are you guys looking into the video recordings for the area?" he asks.

The collar comes to life with a short burst of static. "Rodger, Dodger, but it may take us a right bit of time to locate the right lorry. The camera facing the warehouse has been damaged, probably by Kitn and Johansen to cover their tracks. That means we'll have to chase down every single vehicle leaving the area over the last hour or so, and that will take some time."

Dodger snarls under his breath. "Buggers." He pauses, looking back down the road, then turns to address the collar again. "In the meantime, what do you blokes 'ave on the search aboard the QM2? Have they found anything yet?"

"No, not yet. The Americans loaned us one of their SEAL bomb squads, and they're busy checking out every square inch of the ship, using the unique taggant ID you uncovered, but so far their detectors haven't given off so much as a single peep. It's like the bomb isn't even on the boat."

Dodger nods, thinking. "Hmm. That would jive with what Moose and I were just discussing. If my analysis is correct, the bomb left this area less than an hour ago. That means there's no possible way they could 'ave made it all the way out to sea yet, so my best guess is they 'aven't placed the explosives onboard yet. There may be time to stop them from even getting close to the ship, if we can just figure out exactly how they plan to smuggle the bomb onto the boat past all the security."

"And now past the added security of the American SEAL team, as well. It all seems almost impossible from this end."

"Even considering the combined intelligence and resources of Johansen and Kitn," Dodger agrees, rubbing his head with obvious irritation.

One thing about this conversation has got me confused. "Uh, Dodger, the American humans are more than up to the task of hunting down a bomb on a ship, and they have the added advantage of being fairly inconspicuous. So why would they bother bringing in a bunch of seals to handle all that? I mean, dogs, sure, and maybe even a few cats could manage to get it done in time, but seals? I'm sorry, but in my humble canine opinion those knuckleheads are simply not much use for anything more than barking and belching and balancing a beach ball on the tip of their noses. Everyone knows they're pretty much the circus clowns of the animal kingdom."

Once again Dodger is giving me that strange look I've been seeing for most of the past two days, and he hesitates a bit before responding. "You're joking, right?"

I tell you, I couldn't be more serious about it. And with so many lives at stake and all, and time running out, this is not the right time for a comedy act. So I press him a bit further on the subject. "Look, I understand you Brits have a different way of doing things, and this may come off all politically incorrect or something, but seriously, there comes a time when a dog has to draw the line on all that and put the right canine or even the right human on the job—assuming you can even find a human who's fully up to the task. But seals? Fuggitaboutit! I mean, they're not even fully mammals, just some kind of black furry fish with whiskers. And with brains about the size of a peanut. If that."

Dodger opens his mouth, then closes it, then opens it up again, like he's trying to say something but no words are coming out. Finally he just closes his mouth and looks away, and that seems to help out some with his temporary muteness. It's clear that I've really gotten to him, laying out just how really stupid everyone has been about the whole seal thing.

"Uh, Moose, let's just drop that one for the moment, shall we?" he suggests, which is fine with me, I suppose. Although we really should be arranging to drop a few bloodhounds on the boat, just to be sure. Those noses can pick up just about any scent from miles away.

Just then, the collar comes to life again, interrupting our little discussion on strategy and tactics. "Moose and Dodger, we don't have a bead on the lorry just yet, but one of our cameras appears to have located Mr. Johansen stepping into a flat in Soho. The address is connected to one of his former assistants, a young woman just recently out of university. We have already arranged for a car to take you there, and it should be at your location presently."

"Smashing," Dodger responds, just as a flash of red appears down the road a short ways from us, coming fast. It's Trini and that red Trump spitter sportscar of his!

But just as Trini pulls up in front of us and I'm about to jump in, my collar barks one last time.

"Uh, a slight hiccup in our plans, gents," it says. "We've picked up what is almost unmistakably Mr. Vladimir Kitn, stepping into the Inner Temple at the Inns of Court complex. That's near the Temple Tube station—"

"I know where it is," Dodger snaps, then turns to me, looking suddenly apologetic. "Sorry, I just—I just think this is a bad time to split up our resources, is all, but I don't see as how we 'ave much choice. You'll have to go on to Soho with Trini to track down Johansen while I head to Fleet Street to try and locate Kitn."

All this talk of temples has me confused again. "Kitn's going to temple? Funny, but he doesn't really look Jewish—"

231

Dodger shakes his head at that, a hint of that earlier look returning to his face. "No, Moose, the Temple complex is actually the former London 'eadquarters of the Knights Templar, a group of knights commissioned by the pope during the time of the crusade to guard the ruins of Solomon's Temple in Jerusalem, 'ence the name 'Templar.' And the name of the complex and all the buildings within it. Nowadays the complex is devoted to the study and practice of law." He nods in Trini's direction. "You two better get moving. My guess is Johansen is going to be busy for a while inside that apartment, so I should 'ave just enough time to drop a net on Kitn and still make it back to Soho in time to do the same with our soon-to-be-former PM. In the meantime, don't make any sudden moves unless 'e ends up on the move 'imself."

"Gotcha, boss," Trini tells him, and as I jump into the spitting fire car and he guns the engine, sending gravel flying, I very politely explain to him how I am actually the only Double-O secret agent here, and Dodger is simply my native guide. Just so nobody gets confused about who's really calling the shots on this little mission.

Soho

Now that we've gotten the whole chain-of-command thing straight between us, Trini and I concentrate on finding Johansen's hidey-hole. Supposedly the "flat"—which I take it is an English term for apartment—is just across the way from a hoochy-coochy joint called the Windmill Theater. Which only makes sense, if Johansen is indeed involved in what Trini assures me is an "untoward relationship" with his former assistant. Although I'll admit I did have to have Trini explain what exactly he meant by the word "untoward." And I can't say I'm all that surprised—there is really nothing very "toward" about either of those two boneheads, Johansen and his Russian buddy Kitn.

As we pull to a stop in front of the theater I quickly leap out over the passenger door to the street.

"Wait, Moose," Trini hollers at me. "I thought Dodger said to wait until he got here before—"

I cut him off in mid-sentence. "And I thought we already had that conversation, Sweets. Dodger doesn't give the orders around here, I do. And right now I'm not just going to sit around on my tight tush waiting on some Norch terrier to show up when the man with full knowledge of just what's going on with the bomb is sitting right across the street from us as we speak. Now is our chance to catch him flat-footed with his pants down around his ankles, so to speak. So do we take the chance of his slipping out a back window while we sit here staring at the front door like two puppies at a pet store trying to get adopted? No, not on this dog's watch! This is the point where all my Double-O training takes over and we nab that mangy mutt in fragrant delecto!"

I don't wait for an answer because I don't need one, and instead race across the street dodging the light traffic and wind up at the front door of the apartment complex. Timing my move perfectly, I dash between the legs of an elderly lady just as she opens the door—ignoring her small yelp—and race up the stairs to the second floor. To the tiny private flat where Barkus Johansen lies blissfully unaware that he is soon to be facing his own personal Waterloo. If he isn't in there already.

Soho

I arrive at the door of the apartment slightly out of breath, but that's only to be expected given the fact that my legs are only a few inches in length and therefore have to tackle each step on the stairway with ten times the effort of your standard human, but it forces me to pause and take in the situation. The door to the "flat" is closed and presumably locked, but I see that Johansen's "assistant" has conveniently installed one of those fancy new smart locks. The kind that any preschool kid can hack in a heartbeat. I quickly tap the side of my collar. Which, actually, I realize a bit late is really completely unnecessary, since obviously the guys on the other end are listening in pretty much 24/7 right about now. But hey, tomatoes tomahtoes, right?

I try to keep my voice low in case my quarry is listening in, making sure he isn't unexpectedly interrupted in whatever nefarious activity he's now engaged in. "Uh, collar, could you please—"

"Unlocking now," it says, and I hear the bolt sliding back at that very same moment. I hold back for just a moment, just in case Johansen might have heard it, too, then reach up and gently twist the door knob.

Soho

I swing the door open as easily and noiselessly as I can manage, then slip through into what looks like a very small living area. Whoever this "assistant" is, she clearly isn't pulling down any major bucks. Our itty-bitty main parlor on Helen's boat isn't much smaller than this, and hey, it's a boat.

The room is dark, the curtains drawn over the one tiny window in the back. One open door leads out of the main room to the left—and through it I can see that's the kitchen—and another closed door stands just off to my right. There's light streaming from out from underneath that door, and I can hear muffled voices, one of which I'm quite certain is Johansen and the other a woman, his so-called "assistant" or whatever. My toes are pressed up against something soft, and I look down. It's just a cheap throw rug, off-white and fluffy. Personally I'd never put anything off-white at the very entrance to a house, where everyone tromps in shedding mud and dirt and whatever they've collected on their shoes outside, but whatever. There's just no accounting for taste or common sense any more, you know? And hey, maybe it actually started off stark white and turned off-white over time.

But that rug isn't my problem right now, it's Johansen. And I need to work out a plan on how to make the drop on him. After chewing on the problem a second, I decide to get closer to the door, listen in on whatever's going going on in there, maybe even get a peek through a keyhole or something. I take my first step in that direction—and the whole world falls away underneath me and the room goes completely black!

Soho, One Floor Down

W ell, not completely black, at least not at first. Lying on my back I can barely make out the small square that's been cut out of the floor above me. That mangy off-white rug, that was put there as a trap, and I fell for it. Literally.

When I landed, I must have hit my head, hard, because I'm also seeing a whole planetarium's worth of stars right about now. And then, when I shake my head to clear my vision, I suddenly see his face peering down at me. Johansen. Grinning.

I swing my head on a swivel, trying to find some kind of escape route, but instead all I see are those stars again, and my skull is starting to throb like there's a whole drum corps marching around inside there. I look up again, and Johansen is still there, staring down at me, his evil grin undiminished. "You'll never escape us, Johansen," I lie, desperate for any better alternative right about now. "We've got the whole place surrounded."

Johansen throws his hands up in the air theatrically. "Oh no! I'm so scared! Please don't hurt me, little dog!"

Just then a powerful set of hands latch onto me from behind, and I'm about ready to fight back when a piece of cloth gets pressed tight against my muzzle. A cloth that smells strongly of beets. And something else. Chloroform, I suddenly realize. And then everything goes black again.

Johansen's Secret Evil Lair

I wake up strapped spread-eagled to a metal table in the middle of a sparsely decorated but well-lit room. Above me is some kind of electrical apparatus, equipped with a nozzle or barrel or something that appears to be pointed straight between my legs. I struggle with the cuffs on my forearms, but they refuse to budge, and my head is locked tightly into place with some type of vice, forcing me to stare straight up at the ceiling.

"Electromagnetic restraints, I'm afraid," says a voice somewhere off to my left. Johansen. "And I'm afraid that leads us to a rather inescapable conclusion. You're not going anywhere, my friend. Get it? An inescapable conclusion?"

His maniacal laughter rattles against the walls of the little room. "Funny," I answer, the humor not showing at all in my voice. Seriously, what's with the stupid jokes and all? What kind of dog does that sort of thing, anyway? Certainly not me. I got way too much self-respect for that kind of nonsense.

I shake my head slightly to confirm that the blue collar is still in place around my neck. So at least

M's people can track me. And hear me, assuming that I'm not too far underground to block the signal. So now I've just got to get this joker talking. Spilling the beans on Plan B. "But of course, it doesn't matter what you do to me now does it? It's all over for you now, Johansen. We know all about you and Kitn, and your diabolical plot to blow up the Queen Mary."

He stops laughing. "Blow up the Queen Mary? What in the world are you blabbering on about?"

"Don't be coy with me," I tell him, trying to sound a whole lot braver than I'm feeling right about now. Whoever strapped me onto this table wasn't exactly gentle when he did it, and I can't help but be concerned about that big thingamajig that's hanging right above me, a gizmo that's drawing a bead on the region just south of my private parts right now. "We located the little cottage in Greenwich where the bomb was assembled, and then tracked the bomb to that warehouse in Hackney Wick, leased out under an alias we'll doubtless trace back to you. There's a bomb squad on the Queen Mary defusing the explosives as we speak, and it's only a matter of time before my people burst through these doors and take you into custody, make you answer for all of your perfidious deeds." Suddenly I remember the bit about Johansen having a remote control for the bomb, and I hope I haven't said too much.

But Johansen doesn't seem at all fazed by my remarks. "Honestly, I have no earthly idea what you're prattling on about," he says. I hear a switch being flipped, and the machine above me instantly lights up and starts to hum. "The Queen Mary? Why would we give a farthing about that rusty old scow? Give her a few more years of lumbering back and forth across the Atlantic and she'll likely be relegated to the shipyards to be looted for scrap metal. Or sunk somewhere offshore to serve as ready fodder for the scuba divers and fishes. No, my little canine friend, I'm afraid your accusations are rather insulting. Rather insulting, indeed. Vladimir and I, we could never think that small."

I hear another switch being activated, and now the mystery machine above me is emitting a bright red beam, and I can feel the heat radiating harshly from where it's hitting the metal table in between my toes. It's a laser!

Johansen is still talking. "I'll have to admit, I don't know where you got your information about our plans, but you were close. You see, our target wasn't that little fish, the Queen Mary 2. No, we were aiming at a much bigger fish, indeed. The biggest fish on this island, in fact. In fact, at this very moment, Kitn is completing the installation of our itty-bitty little bomb in one of the new Class 345 trains located in the underground tunnel just beneath Heathrow Airport. The Crossrail tunnel, to be exact, ironically now named the Elizabeth Line. A quite fitting name, indeed."

"You're going to blow up Heathrow?" I ask breathlessly, my eyes locked like laser beams on the laser emitter that is even now boring a hole in the metal table near my feet.

"Heathrow? Blow up a bloody airport? Why, that's already been done a thousand times over. An amateur sport, that one is. No, as I said, our target is much, much bigger. You see, unbeknownst to all but a very few who've been read in to the details—and that short list would include me, the PM, of course—the Elizabeth line has a rather special, top secret offshoot. An offshoot that follows the A4 straight to Barkingham Palace, where our dear Queen is only just arriving to celebrate the birth of her newest great-grandchild with the rest of the Royal Family!"

"No! You're not going to—"

"Oh, but I am," Johansen says with a wicked little chuckle. "You see, it turns out the Queen is preparing a little speech for tomorrow where she is going to announce her formal opposition to Pexit, a move that would almost certainly destroy not only my plans to insure Britain's independence from PETSEC EU, but also my own political career in the bargain. And I'm sure you can understand that I certainly couldn't let that happen. But with the Queen conveniently out of the way, along with her pesky little family and a great many of the human leaders of the UK who will be attending their quaint little celebration, why, by tonight I may just be the most powerful politician in all of England!"

That sets him off again, a shrieking kind of laughter that could possibly shatter a glass if we had one nearby. I glance up, hoping against hope that the sound has managed to break the laser machine, but to my horror I see that the laser beam is now moving! Somewhat slowly, it seems, but the direction is unmistakable. It's heading straight my way!

Johansen's laughter has dropped back down to an evil chuckle. "Ah, I see you now understand the true purpose of my little Dogsplitter device. Now don't be overly concerned about it. I'm actually doing you a big favor, here. I mean, who wouldn't want to have their very own twin brother to share all of life's little joys with? And now I'm going to make that happen for you. Well, to be fair, you won't actually have a *twin* brother. I suppose you could say you'll be more like *half* brothers, right?"

He makes that shrieking noise again, and sweat is now pouring off my forehead and down into my eyes, making it hard to see. Not that I really want to see what's just about to happen, to be honest.

Johansen leans over, and I can finally see his grinning, disgusting face. "Oh, my! Look at the time!" he says, then pulls away again, his voice shrinking slightly as he apparently is walking away. "I do apologize, Agent Moose, but I must be off. I'll be expected back at the residence on Downing Street, what with everything all so up in the air at the palace. Get it? Up in the air? Ha ha ha ha ha!"

And I'm busy trying not to get it when the room suddenly goes black.

Johansen's Secret Evil Lair

I nstantly the electromagnetic shackles on my arms and legs go slack, and the vise holding my head in its iron grip falls away. Even more important, the laser that was about to split me in two is off now, and I take this as a blessed opportunity to leap off the table and put some distance between me and Johansen's Dogsplitter.

"What the—"

It's Johansen, stumbling around in the dark, somewhere off to my left by the sound of things. I drop down on all fours and dash blindly in that direction, hoping to catch him off guard in the darkened confusion. I've only made it a few steps, though, when a brilliant beam of light bursts into the room from the collar around my neck, lighting up the space in front of me like a thousand flashbulbs have just gone off. It's only on for a moment, but it's long enough for me to see Johansen standing in front of me, throwing up his hands to ward it off. And then I'm on top of him, crashing into his chest, my teeth immediately at his jugular.

"I can't see!" he screams, as if that's his biggest problem right now. I'm still trying to work out my next move when the room lights suddenly come back on and the door in front of me crashes open, Dodger and what looks like a dozen canine coppers bursting through the open space to grab Johansen and place him in cuffs. I think I'm still somewhat in a state of shock over everything that's just happened—and I can't seem to ignore the smell of burning metal that still fills the air around me—when Dodger steps in front of me, checking me over quickly from head to toe to make sure I'm not injured.

"Hey, Moose, good work!" he tells me with an ear-splitting grin. "One down, one to go!"

One to go? Oh, right! Johansen may be in custody, but the biggest problem facing us right now is Vladimir Kitn. And the train headed for Barkingham Palace!

I grab Dodger roughly by the shoulders. "Please tell me M has a plan to stop the train from reaching the palace!" I shout, and my collar immediately comes to life.

"Moose, M here. There's no time to waste. The train is already on its way, and everything we've tried so far to stop it or switch it to another track has failed. Johansen evidently took advantage of his security status to override the controls. That means you've got to stop it before it reaches the palace!"

Stop a speeding train loaded to the gills with explosives? I'm really starting to question this whole international dog of mystery career choice. "Okay, what's our next move?" I ask. Dodger starts to answer, but then realizes that I'm talking to the collar, a conversation he's only getting one-sided.

"We don't have enough time to evacuate the Queen and the royal family," M tells me through the collar. "Our only hope is to somehow derail the train before it gets there. And hopefully do so without setting off the bomb."

Which would probably ruin the rest of my plans for the day, I almost tell her. But there's no time to think about any of that. Lives are at stake, and maybe the future of Western civilization, which would explain Vladimir Kitn's involvement in all of this. "I'm on it, but I'm going to need a little in the way of step-by-step instructions here, M. I don't even know where I am."

"You're near Hammersmith, not more than a block from Ravenscourt Park Station. Dodger can show you how to get to the station, and we'll have more for you on the way. Now run!"

I turn to Dodger. "M says we need to get to Ravenscourt Park Station, like immediately."

"Got it!" he tells me, spinning and leading me past all the dog police, out through the door and down a long hall leading, I presume, to the exit. We push through a door to the outside, and I can see that it's nearly night time, the streets filled close to bursting with humans bustling about on their early evening errands. Dodger takes off like a bullet, easily finding a path through all the legs, and in no time we're racing down the steps into the underground.

My collar comes back to life. It's Q'ute this time. "Moose, there should be a sign for the train leading to Ealing."

"Right, I see it," I respond, almost completely out of breath from our mad dash over here.

"Good, follow the signs to that platform, then turn right. At the end of the platform is a small door set into the tiled wall. Go through that. It's an access tunnel leading to the Elizabeth line."

"Ealing," I tell Dodger, pointing out the sign. "Follow me."

We race headlong down the steps to the train for Ealing, causing not a few humans to shout out angrily at us as we brush past. No time for that.

We hit the platform at full tilt, then take a hard right. "I see the door," I inform Q'ute over the collar. "Uh, do you mind putting this thing on speaker mode, so Dodger can hear?"

"Oh, sorry," Q'ute says, and from the way Dodger's looking at me I can see she's already made the switch.

The little access door isn't easy to pry open, but with Dodger and I both pushing and pulling we finally get it open wide enough to squeeze through. The tunnel ahead of us is pitch black.

"Q'ute, you got something on this collar a little less powerful in the way of a flashlight than the one you used on Johansen?" I ask, and immediately the collar emits a brightly focused beam that lights up the path in front of us.

"Okay, Moose, follow the tunnel until you get to another small door. On the other side of that door is the Elizabeth line. And hurry, the train is moving fast, and we only have about a minute before it's past you!"

"Moving as fast as these little Aussie legs will carry me," I reply, breaking into a sprint, Dodger right on my tail. I still don't know how I'm possibly going to stop that train if we can even get to it in time, but for now that's not my problem. I can only assume M and Q'ute have people working on that.

The tunnel turns out to be thankfully short, and Dodger and I throw open the door at the other end and emerge out into another Tube line, a tunnel that looks much nicer than the one we just left. Which only makes sense, since it's apparently brand spanking new and all. In the distance I can hear the unmistakable roar of a train, and it's coming at us fast.

Dodger gives me a wink. "Uh-oh, Moose, sounds like our old friend the dragon is back. Maybe we'd better take cover."

"Funny," I tell him, giving him a sour look that says in an instant how I really feel about his asinine comment. "And just what would a stupid dragon be doing way down here in a subway tunnel, anyway? It's the train, you moron. And from the sound of it, we've got less than a minute left to stop it!"

I tap the side of my collar. "Okay, Q'ute, or whoever's listening. We're here already, standing right next to the tracks. What's next?"

"Hold, please," is what I get back. Not exactly all that useful right about now, and I make no bones letting them know how I feel about it.

"Umm, we're running out of time here, guys. A few suggestions on how to stop the train would be greatly appreciated, you know?" Not for the first time I'm starting to think this collar thing should come with some type of collar ID, you know? Let you know just who exactly you're dealing with in the middle of a life-or-death situation?

"Yeah." It's Q'ute on the line again. Or at least I think it's Q'ute. At least it sounds like her, so I'm not about to argue the point at the moment. "Moose," she/he says, "remember when I told you about the blue collar, about what to do if someone tries to bite you on the neck?"

I do remember that, and as magical as this collar has turned out to be over the past two days, that still makes zero sense to me. "Uh, yeah, what about it?"

"Okay, now, listen to me carefully. You two are standing about twenty feet from where the tunnel veers off to the left slightly, in order to follow the path of the River Thames which is itself just off to your right. Looking in the direction of the palace, that is."

I turn and see it, just as she described. "Okay, and how does that help us?" I can hear the train quite clearly now, and my guess is it's only a matter of seconds before it's upon us.

"Okay, Moose, you've got to trust me here. I need you to lay down on the track with your neck stretched out on the rail nearest you. And do it quickly! You've only got about ten seconds left to get in place!"

"Put my neck—you've got to be kidding me!" I protest loudly over the roar of the train coming down the tunnel.

"No time to argue, Moose, just do it! For God's sake, do it now!" Q'ute screams.

As crazy as it seems, I haven't gotten this far without trusting Q'ute's judgment and the power of this crazy blue collar, and her panicked words spur me to action. Pushing Dodger back up against the wall of the tunnel, I leap forward, thrusting my tiny Aussie head over the nearest rail, the blue collar lined up in the middle of it. Out of the corner of my eye I see the light from the train making the last turn, not fifty feet away from me and closing fast. I squeeze my eyes shut as tight as I can, and say a quick prayer. I only hope Doggie Heaven is every bit as magical as they make it sound. I've just whispered out a final heartfelt "amen" when the front wheel of the train hits my fully exposed neck. And the blue collar.

The Elizabeth Line Tunnel

I'm not exactly sure I have a good grip on how the whole death and resurrection business is supposed to work out, but I'm pretty sure it isn't supposed to play out this way. Okay, well, there is the part about seeing a light at the end of a tunnel and heading that way, but I always imagined that process to be a whole lot quieter. Peaceful, even. And what just happened as the train ran over my neck was anything but peaceful.

"What the—" I can barely hear Dodger's voice over all the mountainous sounds of explosions and rending metal. Did he get killed, too, standing there pressed up against the side of the tunnel? Are we both on our way to Doggie Heaven, now?

"Moose, what in the world just 'appened?" It's Dodger again, and by the sound of things he's somewhere right behind me. I can feel my front paws, which is strange, considering how I'm dead and all, and they seem to be pressed up against something hard and rocky. Slowly I realize that it's the ground. I'm still lying on the ground. In the tunnel. And Dodger is beside me, shaking me.

"Are you okay, Moose?" he asks, in a voice that suggests maybe I'm not. He rolls me over on my back, and I can see his face, shining in the light that's coming from the end of the tunnel. Shining down on us from Heaven.

But then, that's not right. I move my head to see a little better what it's really like on the other side of the tunnel, and as my eyes adjust, it doesn't appear to be anything at all like what I thought Heaven would look like. It's just a river, and a bunch of buildings on the other side. And my neck is killing me right about now, like it just got run over by a train or something. You're not supposed to feel pain like that in Heaven, are you?

Dodger is still shaking me. "Moose, Holy Hannah! What just 'appened? What did you do to the train?"

Okay, that part definitely doesn't line up with the whole Doggie Heaven thing, and as I slowly come to my senses and sit up, I realize that Dodger and I are still somehow magically alive. And sitting here on the floor of the Elizabeth Line tunnel, which doesn't look quite as brand new anymore, by the way. I turn my head again, making my neck scream out like it's being

257

punctured all at once by a thousand tiny knives, and then I see it. A giant hole in the side of the tunnel about twenty or thirty feet away, the pink and orange rays of the setting sun glittering across the River Thames and lighting up the rooftops of the city. And then I hear and feel the sound of a massive explosion going off somewhere in the distance, somewhere on the other side of the hole, and the Thames instantly erupts with a giant spray of water like a regular Niagara Falls that's running in reverse.

Sickbay, The Tower Of London

All in all, I guess I'm in pretty good shape, considering I've just recently been run over by a speeding, out-of-control subway train. My neck is feeling a bit bruised, but PETSEC's docs say there's no permanent damage. And I still have no idea what just happened back there in the tunnel.

M has just arrived at the Tower, and I can see the concern painted all over her well-lined face as her eyes carefully explore what's left of mine. "Moose, I just talked to your veterinary surgeon, and she said—"

"Yeah, M, I'm fine. I'm not that easy to put down after all, I suppose. And you know, stopping that crazy thing with my own neck on the line like that, well, that's something I've kind of been *training* for all of my life, heh-heh. But hey—"

M doesn't look at all amused, which is kind of a downer, right? I mean, I've been saving that line for several hours, just waiting for a chance to slide it into a conversation. But I guess some people just weren't born with a sense of humor, you know? Especially the Brits. If it ain't some dumb guy getting slapped with a pie in the face, or stepping on a rake and getting slammed in the face, or maybe just some guy mugging a stupid looking face into the camera, the English don't seem to get it.

M is patting the bed impatiently with one paw as she finally speaks up. "Yes, well, I bet you have a million questions right about now. Okay, then, let's start with the collar. You probably already know Q'ute had a ton of little tricks stashed away inside of that little thing. Well, one of those tricks involved the material it was made out of, a type of metal called a memory alloy. The collar itself was formed by bending a thin metal thread into neat little loops, over and over, like a tightly coiled spring. But the metal that made up those loops still somehow remembered how it was originally shaped, a metal thread that was forged in one long line, like an arrow. An arrow that originally stretched out almost a mile in length, as it turns out. Now normally the collar would retain its new coiled shape, but under certain stresses—like the stress of being compressed, for example—it would automatically respond by expanding ever so slightly, regaining to some degree or another a little of its original linearity. The true brilliance in how the collar was crafted was that the expansion forces were largely in direct proportion to the amount of compression forces being applied to it. Bite down on the collar, for example, and you'd wind up with a mouthful of metal, your jaws pried wide open. But if the collar experienced a much stronger force, like the force of an entire train pressing down on it, why the expansion forces would be commensurately greater, don't you see."

Wow. "You mean—"

"Yes, Moose, when the wheel of the train rolled up on top of your collar, the metal tried to respond by returning completely to its original shape, a mile long strip of metal. Except that it couldn't, really, because the wheel of the train was in the way. So instead it simply tossed that wheel up out of the way, giving it all the room it needed to fully expand."

Now it's all starting to make sense. Sort of. "I see. So the hole in the tunnel wall—"

"Was caused by the train crashing through at a point where the wall was the thinnest, running slightly above ground right next to the Thames."

"And the explosion I heard—"

"Was caused by the bomb Kitn had placed in the train finally detonating, right on time. And, fortunately for everyone involved, right in the very wrong location. Well, at least as far as Kitn was concerned."

"So the palace—"

"Yes, the palace was saved, along with everyone in it. Including the Queen and the Royal Family, all thanks to you, my dear Moose. An act of bravery unmatched in the annals of British history, but unfortunately an act that very few will ever hear about, lest the secret of our presence at the palace and our role in protecting the Royals should leak out."

I suddenly realize I'm blushing. "Well, I'm not really all that much for—"

"Nevertheless, you should know that the Queen is quite pleased with your valor, and she intends to thank you personally for everything you've done for England. And for her family."

"Shucks. Just all in a day's work. All part of why they call us *secret* agents, I suppose."

"Yes. And rightly so. But still, not quite a secret to those of us at the highest levels of our government." She pauses and surreptitiously checks her watch.

"Well, it's good to see you've come through all this without any serious injuries. We'll chat again very soon, but for the moment I have my hands full dealing with all of the collateral fallout of this whole mess. Mr. Johansen is safely behind bars, now, but I'm sorry to say that Mr. Kitn is still on the lam, as you Chicagoans are wont to say. And of course we still need to handle all the media spin on why a train crashed through the wall of the new underground line from Heathrow and wound up in the river."

The river. That reminds me. "When the bomb went off, did anyone—"

"No, Moose, thankfully not a single soul was injured in the explosion, which is a miracle, I suppose, given all the traffic that goes up and down the Thames every day. A few boats were damaged by the geyser, though, although I suspect any concerns about that will be more than assuaged by the size of the checks we'll be handing out to their owners in compensation." Her eyes drop back down to her watch again. "Oh, dear, look at the time! I must be off! But we'll be in touch over the next few days about the ceremony with the Queen. I personally wouldn't miss that for the world."

I nod at her as she turns gracefully and heads out the door. My neck is already feeling much better, but what's really pressing hard on me at the moment is the emptiness in my belly as I realize I haven't really had anything substantial to eat the whole day. I stop a nurse who's busy looking at my chart. "Uh, you guys wouldn't possibly have a cafeteria around here by any chance—"

She shakes her head. "No food or drink until tomorrow morning, I'm sorry to say. Doctor's orders."

Hmph. Doctor or no, there's no way this dog is waiting until tomorrow to grab a few kibbles to help get me through the night. But what the doctor doesn't know can't hurt me, so I decide to keep my peace for the time being.

I tap Nursie on the arm again. "Uh, okay, but hey, are you guys done poking and prodding me, here? Am I free to go?" I look around the room for my belongings, and I suddenly realize something's missing. The bright blue collar. After it tossed the train in the air I guess it must have basically self-destructed. But now, without any kind of collar at all, I'm starting to feel a little naked all of a sudden. Exposed.

The nurse sees me rubbing my neck and smiles. "I'm told the staff back in Chicago has located your old collar and is having it expedited by overnight air. A courier should deliver it to you first thing in the morning."

Huh. Well, that's a relief. Still, I've kind of gotten used to Q'ute's magical blue collar. Although the less-than-a-dollar collar is kinda comforting, too, in its own little way. "Uh, is there any way I can get some kind of replacement lined up for my blue collar?" I ask, crossing my toes.

The nurse looks confused. "Blue collar? Why would any self-respecting dog want to wear a blue collar? My lord, you'd stand out like a sore paw with something like that hanging around your neck." She gives me a little cluck, then sets my chart down on a side table and sashays out the door.

Stand out? I think back on how all the humans have treated me over the past two days with that blue collar hanging on me, taking one quick look at it and then just as quickly looking the other way, pretending they didn't even see me in the first place. And that may actually have been the collar's neatest trick of all. It's like I was wearing a collar of invisibility the whole time. Go anywhere I want, do anything my heart desires, and never give a second thought to anyone trying to bite my head off. Except for Bella, of course. I don't think even the blue collar could protect me from that sharp tongue of hers.

Speaking of which, naked or not, it's well past time to head for home. It's been a long two days, and this doggie desperately needs a nappie right about now. Oh, and some kibble. Can't forget about that. I wonder for the very first time if the mutt they assigned to the boat as my stand-in has had the good sense to keep his filthy chops off my din-din...

Limehouse Marina

t's been almost two weeks since my life turned into a regular train wreck, and to be honest, I don't really miss all the excitement. We met the Queen, and that was pretty cool, I suppose, getting knighted and all. Huh, Sir Moose McGillicutty. It kind of has a nice ring to it, don't you think?

Bella and I have settled back into our normal two-meal-a-day routine, interspersed by nappies and the occasional walkie, mostly just a long lap around the marina. My mistress Helen has been busy with phone calls and errands and last-minute darts out the door, and we haven't seen my master Howard for weeks—not that that is much of a loss. I get the feeling he's not really much of a dog lover. Or even a cat lover, for that matter. He's more like just a Howard lover, in my humble canine opinion, you know? He barely even bothers to check in with Helen these days, and I get the sense she's not missing it all that much.

It's turned a little chilly outside, especially sitting on the water and all, so after breakfast Bella and I decide to curl up peacefully next to the coal burning space heater in the main parlor—although why they call that thing a space heater is beyond me, because it doesn't look at all very space agey to me, more like something drug in from the stone age. I've almost completely drifted off into that wonderful place where bicycles can't outrun me when suddenly Helen's cell phone starts buzzing on the kitchen counter, and she rushes in out of the bedroom to grab it.

"Hello, this is Helen McGillicutty. How may I help you?" she says, somewhat breathlessly. "Oh! Mrs. Friedman! It's good to hear—Yes, I can—No, absolutely, I understand the urgency—Of course, I'll be there right away!"

She hangs up the phone and beams down at us with the biggest smile I think I've ever seen on her. And certainly the only smile I've seen her wearing since the day we left Chicago.

"Listen up you two," she tells us even more breathlessly. "I have to step out for a moment and see a woman about an—opportunity. I'll only be gone for a little while. You two try not to get into any trouble while I'm gone." She stops and looks down at me rather pointedly. "And that means you, Moose. You naughty little mischief maker!"

She's trying to give me a scolding look, but somehow she can't seem to suppress that ginormous smile she's wearing, so of course it doesn't really work. Like it ever would, anyway. I just reward her with a yawn and a little wiggle of my tail, while Bella gives her that trademark puppy-dog-innocent look of hers. You'd think it would start to wear on humans after a while, but somehow it seems to work every time. Humans are all so simple minded and gullible, in the end.

Helen plucks up her purse and gloves and races out the door, only stopping to lock it behind her before she leaves. Like that really makes any difference—anyone who tries to come through that door unwanted would have me to deal with, in the flesh. And as you know, I'm licensed to kill.

"A little while" to Helen turns out to be the rest of the day, and it's already well past dinner time when she finally gets back home. Normally that would pose some serious logistical problems for a dog locked up on a tiny little boat, having no back yard and all, but Helen found a piece of some type of artificial grass that she placed out on the bow of the boat just past the doggie door, and after a few hit-and-slightly-miss tries,

269

Bella and I have finally gotten used to it. Of course, most of the slightly miss bit was largely due to Bella—with that overlarge Corgi butt of hers, it took her a while to get the hang of just where the edge of the grass was. Hang being the operative word, here.

Anyway, to make up for leaving us alone all day, Helen had stopped by the butcher's on her way home and picked up some special treats for us for din-din, a few nice fatty pieces of meat and two delicious cow bones. I can only wonder why she didn't bother to get a bone for Bella.

"Eat up," Helen tells us as she lays our dinner bowls out on the tile floor in the kitchen. "We'll need to get to bed early tonight. Tomorrow's going to be a big day!"

Personally, I don't have to be encouraged to get to bed early. Lying in a nice cozy bed curled up next to Helen is pretty much the definition of heaven for me. Except for when Howard's around, with all his snoring and thrashing around. But like I said, he's been AWOL for weeks, so bedtime's back to being my favorite part of the day.

And Helen wasn't kidding about the big day part. The next morning we're up well before daybreak, like we actually have some place to go or something. Breakfast is a rushed affair—but then I'm not really one to linger over a bowl of delicious chow, now, am I?—and before I know what's happening it's all leashes on collars and dashing out the door.

Like I said, it's starting to get a bit nippy outside, especially this early in the morning, so I'm really starting to appreciate the fact that Helen took the time to slip a nice wool sweater on me. Despite what I said earlier about purse doggie outfits. I look over at Bella, who's shivering just a bit in the cold, but then, hey, like I said, every time someone tries to put a sweater on Bella she just freezes up and refuses to move a muscle, like someone sprayed liquid nitrogen or something on her. So that's all on her, as far as I'm concerned. Well, now that I think about it, more like *not* on her, am I right?

Meanwhile, Helen's moving along the path by the water like she's got someplace else to be, and it's all my short little legs can do to keep up. We quickly pass the turnoff for the walkway running along the canal toward the north, then we reach the parking lot underneath the tracks for the Overground station. And much to my surprise, what do I see but my old friend Trini, this time driving a snazzy looking black sedan!

"Sweet Chocolate!" I bark, and Bella looks at me like I've gone bonkers or something. But then I remember, Bella's never met Trini before. She was stuck back at the palace the whole time Dodger and I were dashing around London, trying to track down Kitn, Johansen and the bomb.

"Hush, Moose!" Helen tells me, waving her hand in my direction like she's patting at the air. "If you keep making a fuss like that, he'll never give us a ride." She looks up at Trini. "Um, I don't quite know what's got into him, he's not normally like that. I promise you he'll sit quietly on my lap in the backseat the whole time and you won't hear a peep out of him."

"No worries," Trini assures her, flashing that brilliant white smile of his. "I like dogs. Better than most people, actually. We'll get along just fine."

"Well, uh, thank you. That's very kind." She opens the back door and Bella and I hop right in. Helen's just about to join us when suddenly she remembers something. "My purse! I must have left it back on the boat!"

"Not a problem," Trini says. "I got no place better to be. The dogs and I will just wait here at the curb while you go back and get it."

Helen smiles back at him, although it's a twisted little smile. I can tell she's got something on her mind that's got her a bit rattled. "Okay, you two," she tells us, shutting the car door. "You wait here. I'll be right back." She starts to turn away, but then looks back at us. "And Moose—"

I know the drill. Stay out of trouble. No mischief out of you, naughty boy. Yeah, yeah. I've heard that line so much she doesn't even have to say anything to me anymore, just give me that look, so I simply settle myself down in the back seat, tucking my paws up under me. That seems to mollify her, and finally she takes off, almost running back down along the pier to our boat.

As soon as she's out of earshot I sit back up and swing my muzzle in Bella's direction. "Hey, Trini, meet my good friend Bella. Bella, this is Trini. He gave Dodger and I a few rides here and there when we were trying to pin down Kitn and Johansen."

Something seems to click in Bella's eyes as she finally understands the connection. "Nice to meet you,

273

Mr. Trini," she woofs. "But—do you actually understand Doglish? How? I've never heard of a human—"

I pat her on the back lightly. "It's a long story, Bella, but I'll fill you in on it later." I know the details are probably still very painful and fresh to Trini, so I try to spare him the unnecessary rehash. I turn back to face him. "The real question is, how did you manage to pick up this fare in the first place? I didn't make the Uber call, Helen did. And I'm not even wearing the blue collar anymore. That whole collar thing kind of blew up in my face when we had to stop the bomb."

"Yeah, I heard," Trini says. "The whole story is running more or less on a constant loop on the PetUK channel these days. But about your first question, PETSEC managed to hack some kind of override into Uber's network, so now I get first dibs on any rides your mistress requests. Got to be a little careful with that, or she might start getting suspicious. After all, I'm not exactly unforgettable, you know." He flashes his smile again and puffs out his chest. "But anyway, Moose, this call came in with a special request that I take along two little dogs, so it was pretty much a no-brainer that you and your Corgi friend were involved."

Interesting. "And, uh, not to sound cheap or unappreciative, but is PETSEC still picking up the charges?" I ask.

"Not for this ride, little buddy. Otherwise your mistress Helen would really start to get suspicious." He stops and digs around in his pocket for something. "Oh, by the way, I'm supposed to give you two these little radios." He reaches out and attaches a small flat silvery object to the back of my dog tag, then does the same for Bella. "You can use these in an emergency to contact headquarters. Or even if the two of you just need a ride somewhere. You never know. Especially since folks like Vladimir Kitn are still on the loose. It's a dark, dangerous world out there."

I can't see my radio, since it's hanging around my neck, but I lean over to check out Bella's. "You mean this little thing is like a blue collar? How did they manage to miniaturize it—"

"It's not a blue collar," he explains, "just the radio part. It can make calls, or connect you up with headquarters, but that's all, no expanding coils or other crazy tricks. And unlike the blue collar it's designed to

275

be mostly unnoticeable, so it won't let you sneak in and out of places like the collar did, with the humans looking the other way. Although, given the nonstop coverage you guys are getting on PetUK, I'm sure it will be quite some time before anyone in a position of authority in London forgets those two cute little pusses of yours."

I'm not all that sure I like my face being referred to as a cat, but I am somewhat relieved to hear my dog tags won't be blowing up on me anytime soon. And I wouldn't mind trying out the whole sneaking-past-the-humans thing again. I can still almost taste that one amazing meal Dodger and I had in the cafeteria under that big watchtower clock.

Trini is looking out my window, down the pier toward our boat. "Uh, it's ix-nay on the alk-tay for now," he murmurs under his breath. "Boss lady is back."

Sure enough, as I turn to see where he's looking, Helen is already opening the car door and sliding in. She must have been running the entire time, judging from how heavy she's breathing.

"Thanks for waiting," she says, slipping on her safety harness and in pretty much the same move scooping me up into her lap, her purse landing on the seat beside us. "That was unfortunate. I was already running a bit late, so if you don't mind, Columbia Road, driver. And step on it!"

Trini's Uber

I must say, I can't imagine anyone better suited for driving a car than Trini. He really seems to love it, and his reflexes are amazing. He's got the little sedan darting in and out of the morning rush hour traffic almost as nimbly as he handed the Trump spittle sportscar. I look up at Helen and she's turned almost white, her right hand gripping the handle on the side of the door in a death grip. But she's not saying anything. Wherever it is we're heading, getting there on time must be almost as important to her as life itself.

As for me, she's got her left arm draped around my body protectively, her left hand clenched tightly on my collar, so I'm not going anywhere, regardless of how much the car is lurching. Bella's dropped down into the floor well, her bulky Corgi body filling in the space almost perfectly.

With all of the bouncing back and forth, I'm finally settling into a good rhythm, and my eyelids are starting to get rather heavy. It was an early morning, you know, so hey, no judging, okay? A dog needs his sleep if he's to be counted on when push comes to shovel, you know?

Anyway, Trini has just made this one truly impressive maneuver, impressive even for him, shooting between two cars and immediately making a turn onto a deserted side street, and I can tell by the GPS screen on his dash that we're getting really close to our mysterious final destination, when suddenly I hear a loud popping sound from somewhere right in front of us, like a car backfiring or a gun going off really, really close, and then without warning the entire front windshield explodes inward in a hail of glass!

Trini's Uber

Curse words start flying out of Trini's mouth like we're at a drunken sailor's convention, and immediately the sedan starts lurching wildly from side to side. "Get down!" Trini screams in our general direction, and immediately Helen tries to drop down into the empty space beside us. But her seatbelt won't let her, so she lets go of me and the door handle just long enough to unbuckle it, then dumps me down onto the floorboards, safe and sound, and throws herself down after me. I can't see a thing from my vantage point down on the floor of the car, with Helen draped on top of me and all, but I gather from Trini's expletive filled muttering and the violent way he's handling the sedan that the whole windshield-exploding thing was just as much a surprise to him as it was to me.

"What's happening?" I holler out over the noise of the tires squealing, the engine revving and the wind flooding in through the open windshield. And did I mention Helen's nonstop screaming?

"It's Kitn!" Trini hollers back in anguished Doglish, his staccato barks cutting through all the clatter around us, and as scared as Helen is right now, I'm sure she doesn't even notice it. "He took a shot at us just as I turned onto that side street back there. I think he was aiming for my head, and only missed because he wasn't expecting me to make the turn just at that moment."

I manage to squeeze out from underneath Helen, who's busy right now trying to make herself as small and as low as possible. I risk a quick peak out the back window, and sure enough, it's the Russian, riding shotgun in a large black sedan, his head and a pistol hanging out the side window, the business end of the pistol pointed our way. Every now and then he gets off a shot, but so far Trini's crazy gyrations are managing to make us a hard target to hit. And thank Dog for that.

"Moose!" Trini yells at me from the front seat. "The radio! Call it in! We need reinforcements, and fast!"

In all the excitement I had almost forgotten it, the dog tag radio! Of course! I tap it, and can barely hear the sound of it coming alive over all of the squealing and revving and screaming. "PETSEC, this is Double-O-Ten. Moose. We've got a situation, here. Vladimir Kitn is on our tail, and it looks like he's got a view to a kill. And that view's getting closer by the moment."

"Roger that, Ten," comes the voice from the dog tag, and if I didn't have world-class canine ears, I don't think I could have heard a word of it over all the ruckus. "We've got you located, and we'll have help to you in under a minute. Hold tight! Help is on the way!"

Just then a bullet hits our rear window, and it explodes as well, raining glass once again all over the inside of the car. At least it's apparently safety glass, because otherwise we'd have been cut to shreds by all the shards flying around the tiny compartment. A problem not helped at all by Trini's wild roller coaster maneuvers, which has me bouncing around the back seat like a regular pool ball. I grab onto the door handle with one paw and hold on for dear life. "You better make it quicker than that," I yell at my collar. "Or else stop and pick up four caskets to take us home in! Two of them human size!"

"Incoming," my collar answers, and instantly I hear a loud whining sound drifting through the shattered back window, directly behind us. I sneak another peek out the window, risking getting some random glass particles in my eyes, and see a black helicopter just like the one back in Greenwich barreling down on Kitn's car. Suddenly there's a bright flash from the right side of the copter, and the next thing I know a tiny fire-spitting missile swoops down through Kitn's own rear window and detonates!

Trini's Uber

T rini has somehow managed throughout the entire crazy car chase through the crowded streets of London to keep one good eye on the road in front of him and another eye fixed on the car that's been pursuing us, so just like me he sees Kitn's black sedan explode in a huge ball of fire and fury, and then flip way up into the air and land off to one side of the street like it had just been swatted aside by a giant hand. With the danger from our rear flank now apparently well behind us, he finally takes his foot off the gas, makes another quick turn and pulls us off to the side of the road as well.

"Hiro and Wolf," he says, turning around with his trademark alabaster grin showing as Helen slowly pushes herself up from the floorboards. Well, he may in fact be grinning, but I can't help but notice the slight tremor that's sounding in his voice.

Helen's tremor isn't small at all, and neither is her voice. It's more like a large volcano going off inside the car. "What in the Sam Hill was that all about?" she demands in a very loud voice. I think her ears must be ringing every bit as much as mine are right now, which may explain some of the volume. But not all of it, not by a long shot.

I look down at Bella, and she's still tucked down in the floorboards, trembling like she's having some kind of fit. "It's okay," I assure her, even though I don't actually feel all that assured myself at the moment. Out the missing back window of the car I can see our little black helicopter taking one last low pass over our heads, and my dog tag phone comes back to life. "Looks all clear from up here," the voice says, a voice I imagine is being relayed in from the copter. "Bogies down. You blokes might want to send in a cleanup crew, though. You've got an entire street full of very angry and confused humans milling around down there. Extremely angry and confused, in fact, judging from the looks of things up here."

I know I have to take command of trying to straighten out things on this end, but I still take a second to put in a word for the good guys. "Hey, by the way, thanks, HQ. And you guys up in the air. I really thought we were goners for a second there."

"Yeah, well, sorry it took us so long, good buddy," says the helicopter voice. "But we had to stop off for some crumpets and tea along the way. A dog can't be going into battle on an empty stomach, you know. Wouldn't be prudent."

"Roger that," I answer with a small nervous laugh, then turn my attention back to Helen and Bella. Helen is shaking visibly as she glances around at all the destruction both inside the car and out and repeats her earlier question.

"What in tarnation was that all about?" she asks Trini, leaning heavily over the seat in front of her.

"Sorry, ma'am," he answers, winking. "But you did say to step on it, after all. And I got you here with full on five minutes to spare!"

"Why, I never!" Helen struggles to find the door handle—which only minutes ago had seemed to be almost permanently attached to her right hand—then finally manages to open the door, shushing me out. "Don't think you're going to get a good review from me after all that, young man! In fact, I imagine you'll be lucky to even keep your license after that fiasco of a ride!"

While Helen is talking I take the time to examine the back of our little sedan, which is now completely riddled with bullet holes from one side of the car to the other. Thanks to Trini we somehow managed to survive Kitn's dastardly attack, but apparently we only escaped by the very skin of our teeth. Which, by the way, is another human phrase I've never quite understood. Teeth have skin?

I'm distracted from my thoughts by the sight of Bella flopping out of the back of the car, her little legs all wobbly, and I suddenly remember that while Bella has heard all about my own daring exploits in the field, and even managed to survive that one chase through the halls of Barkingham Palace, she's never really had to face any real danger quite on the scale of this last little outing of ours. I rush over to comfort her, but I know it will likely take a great many weeks before she can possibly put it all behind her. Maybe even months.

Suddenly, I catch a familiar scent in the air, and almost immediately I start sneezing and wheezing. Flowers! Looking up and down the street I spot a veritable army of flower vendors setting up shop in the middle of the road, filling up the entire street with giant buckets of—fresh flowers! I clamp one paw over my nose and try to focus on mouth breathing. Is this what Helen's big surprise was all about? Bringing me to a flower market, for Dog's sake? And a flower market on steroids, at that! What in the world was she thinking?

"Oh, Moose," Helen tells me, bending down and gently stroking my head. "You poor thing. I completely forgot that they turn Columbia Road into one giant flower market on Sundays. And the biggest flower market in London, I hear. You must be absolutely miserable. We have to get you safely inside and away from all of this." Her voice comes out sounding pretty angry, but I know it's not directed at me. If anything, maybe my problems are kind of helping the situation a bit. You know, helping her focus on something other than our almost getting killed and all.

Meanwhile, in between my heroic sneezes, Trini has evidently read the writing on the wall and knows that it's well past high time to make with his goodbyes. Before the coppers all swarm in and start asking some uncomfortable and largely unanswerable questions. I can already hear their sirens in the distance as he throws me a smart parting wave and a wink and drives off, this time at a far less frenetic pace.

Back on the sidewalk, Helen is still fuming, but then she turns and sees the storefront beside us and seems to transform somehow, a little of her fury venting off almost visibly, returning her to her usual stoic Midwestern resolve. She reaches down to straighten her skirt, then checks her hair in the reflection from a nearby plate glass window. "Well, not exactly ideal, but I've been through worse, I suppose," she says, the steely grit slowly returning to her voice. I give off a small woof and jump up onto her legs to try and make her feel better, and while she does manage to push me down firmly and tells me to sit, I can see the tiniest little smile starting to creep back into the corners of her mouth. She looks up at the number painted onto the side of the shop just above our heads. "146 Columbia Road. Well, Moose, I guess it's time for us to go inside and face the music. Come on, you two rascals!" And with that, and with another small straightening of her skirt, she opens the front door of the shop and marches inside.

Hiro + Wolf

Almost as soon as we step inside we're met by this very pretty lady with dark glasses, brown and blonde streaked hair hanging softly almost halfway down her back, and maybe the brightest set of red toenails I think I've ever seen. And believe me, from my vantage point I've seen a lot of toenails.

"My goodness, Helen, it's so dear of you to come rushing over like this at the last minute, with almost no warning. All day yesterday, and now so very early this morning," the shopkeeper says, smiling. "And my goodness, all that noise outside this morning! I don't think I've ever heard the flower vendors raise such a commotion. A few minutes ago it sounded just like a bomb going off out there. Rattled all the windows, it did." She helps Helen with her jacket, hanging it on a small hook on the wall just behind the cash register before returning. "And just look at the two of you," she beams, bending down for a moment to scratch both of us behind the ears. Always appreciated, I can assure you. Especially from the ladies. She glances up at Helen with a smile. "I take it your trip over here from the marina was uneventful?"

Helen smiles back, although it's a crooked little smile. "It had its ins and outs, I suppose, but at any rate we made it here in one piece."

"Well, I can't tell you how much Amy and I appreciate your helping us out like this. When I first got word that we'd won the trip, I was so excited, but then I thought about all the logistical issues, leaving the business behind for well over three weeks, and it was all I could do to put it all together in time. Then my entire crew suddenly comes down with the flu the day before Amy and I were scheduled to leave for Athens, and—"

"So you called me in to help out, Bee," Helen says. "And I'm sorry about everyone having the flu, but I'm happy to have the chance to do something useful for a change. To get away from the boat and meet some fresh new faces for once. Thank you so much for thinking of me."

"No, no, the thanks are all mine. The thing is, as hard as Amy and I have been working lately, this trip couldn't have come at a better time. We really need to get away from all this, even if for only a short time, just to refresh our batteries."

Helen nods, smiling. "And as much as I'm rapidly losing interest in being stuck onboard a boat, I really envy the two of you. Three whole weeks cruising around the entire Mediterranean, stopping off at every major archeological and historical site along the way, not to mention the shows. And the food!"

"And all of it curated by several distinguished professors of antiquity from Cambridge University, no less," the shopkeeper adds enthusiastically. What did Helen say her name was? Bee? Well, that certainly explains the brown and yellow hair. She's still talking. "Well, all I can say is, it's a once in a lifetime opportunity for us, and without your stepping in here to help out, it would have all been wasted." She pauses. "But, about the pay—"

Helen shakes her head with a fiercely determined look on her face. "No, don't even think about it for one moment. After all, it's just three short weeks, and it will all be great fun for me. Besides, like I told you, while my husband has a permit to work in this country, that doesn't exactly come with the same privileges for me. But money isn't all that much of an issue for me, anyway, and I think babysitting the shop might help recharge my own set of batteries, you know? While I figure out what to do with my life going forward. Now that Howard, you know—"

Bee steps over and drapes an arm around Helen's shoulders. "Oh, let's not get the cart before the horse on that one quite yet, shall we? All marriages go a bit pear-shaped every now and then, and you know you really shouldn't pay all that much attention to all those Chinese whispers. Just give it time, and I'm sure it will all work out in the end."

Helen now has a small tear leaking down her cheek, and Bee reaches over the counter, grabbing a tissue from underneath and quietly handing it to Helen.

"I'm so sorry," Helen finally squeaks out. "I shouldn't be troubling you with all my problems, especially just as you're leaving on your big adventure."

"It's no trouble at all, my dear," Bee assures her. "We all go through it at one time or another. But I think you're right about needing something more constructive to do to take your mind off all that. Idle hands are the Devil's playpen, you know." Bee pauses and looks thoughtful for a second. "You know, Amy and I have been thinking of possibly opening up another shop, and if things work out over the next few weeks, maybe we could talk about that a little more when we return from holiday."

"That would be lovely," Helen says, her mood seeming to brighten just a bit. She glances around the shop, taking in all the brightly colored collars and leashes and bowties and such. Picking up one collar from the counter in front of her, she holds it up to the light. "Oh, this one is quite striking. Is it new?"

"As a matter of fact it is," Bee says, rather proudly it seems to me. "Part of our newest collection. We had planned to launch it later this week, but now Amy and I are thinking we should put it off until we return. Part of the excitement of running a business like this is seeing how our regular customers react to our newest designs, you know?"

"I understand completely," Helen says, setting the collar back down. "Although I can't wait to see how that would look on my little Bella. She's quite the show horse, you know. Or I suppose I should have said show dog."

As the two women laugh lightly at Helen's pathetic little joke I can't help but think how little of a show dog Bella really is. I mean, she likes getting a new collar every now and then just like pretty much any other dog, but anything beyond that and she becomes a virtual statue. I remember one Halloween when Helen dressed her up like a hot dog, complete with fake ketchup and mustard, and she stood in one spot for almost an hour before Helen finally took pity on her and pulled it off.

Me, on the other hand, I clean up nicely. Put a dandy new outfit on me and I'm ready to paint the town red. But, of course, that would be silly, wouldn't it? Who really wants the town painted red, anyway? And I'd probably wind up getting some of the paint on my new outfit, which would kind of defeat the entire purpose, am I right?

Another woman has joined us, a taller, blonde woman, equally as lovely as Bee—in a human sort of way, that is—and Bee has now moved over to stand beside her. "Amy, I'd like you to meet Helen, the American woman I told you about who's agreed to keep watch over our little shop while we're gone. Or at least until everyone gets over the flu."

"That's so sweet of you," Amy says. "I guess we could have just closed this store down until everyone recovers, but Bee tells me you expressed such a strong interest in the place, that you've already been in here several times, shopping for your two little sweethearts. And apparently you have some experience with retail—"

"Oh, yes," Helen gushes. Maybe overgushes a little, but hey, who am I to judge? "Well, not exactly with a pet clothing store, but I did help manage a small dress shop all the time I was going to college. I paid my way through school that way."

Amy shakes her head, smiling. "Well, I think you'll find this to be far less complicated. Our inventory is rather limited, by comparison, and almost everything is one size fits all. Other than the collars, of course. And, if you have any questions, you can just always call the other store. They'll be more than happy to help out."

"Plus, if it ever gets to be too much to handle, you can just lock down the till and walk away," Bee adds. "And of course, the staff here at Artisans and Adventurers should be able to fill in if there's ever an emergency."

"I'm sure everything will be fine," Helen tells them, checking her watch. "But hey, look at the time!

You two had better get moving if you're going to make your flight."

"Of course," Amy says, taking one last wistful look around the little shop. "And remember, if anything comes up you don't think you can handle, anything at all, you have our cell numbers. Don't hesitate to give us a tinkle."

"And ruin your well-deserved vacation?" Helen laughs. "I wouldn't think of it! And after spending an entire day here with Bee running the shop, I can't imagine I'll run into any hiccups at all with this, not in three short weeks. After all, it's all just a matter of showing the customers all your wonderful designs, then taking their credit cards or cash and making change. That's the easiest part of running a business, not anything at all like the challenges of designing new products or the drudgeries of keeping the books. I'll be just fine." She makes a shooing gesture with her hands. "Now be off, the both of you. Have fun. Don't give this place another thought until you're back home safe and sound."

Helen walks them to the front door, shooing them outside, while Bella and I take the opportunity to check out the place, sniffing around for any secret messages some other dog might have left behind. Maybe Hero, or even Woof, the two dogs I'm assuming the store is named after. I sure hope I'll get a chance to meet them sometime soon. They must be pretty interesting fellas, for humans to have bothered to create a whole business around them and all.

I'm in the middle of sniffing out a particularly intriguing odor when Helen comes back, spinning around in little circles on her tiptoes. Sorta like I do when I get really excited. "Okay, you two," she says, and I can tell right away the teary-eyed moment is well behind us now. In fact, the look she's giving us right now is absolutely—radiant, I guess you'd call it. Like the look she used to give my master Howard, back in the day when I was still just a puppy. Back when he used to bring fresh flowers home almost every day. Back when he used to come home at all, for that matter.

But, in hindsight, that was a big mistake. Thinking about flowers, that is. Fresh flowers, at that. And it immediately sends me off into another sneezing fit.

"You poor little thing," Helen says, leaning over to stroke the top of my head. "What in the world was I thinking? I forgot all about the flower market, and how that affects you. Even indoors, apparently, and even with the doors closed. I guess I'll just have to leave you at home on Sundays from now on. Or see someone about those allergies of yours."

See someone? A vet? No, I'd rather take my chances with the roses, thank you very much. Seeing a doctor is pretty much the last item on my bucket list these days. My bottom itches like the dickens just thinking about it. All those cold glass thermometers. And the shots, don't forget about the shots. I'm sure anything they might have for my—what did she call it, agonies?—would come with a whole neck full of painful shots. Or at least some foul-tasting pills. No, I'll just take my chances hanging out on the boat all by myself one day a week, thank you very much.

And that will actually work out pretty well in my favor. It'll give me a chance to check in with M once a week in person, see if she has any interesting new assignments for me. And while I'm out there hanging around the Tower, looking for work, there's no reason I can't also check in with that lovely canine assistant of hers. A certain Afghan Hound named Moneypenny. A boyfriend, you say? Bah! He doesn't stand a chance, that one, not by a long shot. Not when stacked up against a bona fido Double-O Knight of the Realm secret agent. And an agent with a license to kill, at that. Not that I'd ever use it for the wrong reasons... But did I mention that Moneypenny is *really* good looking?

Helen is busy flitting about the store, straightening things and dusting and humming happily to herself. Bella's found herself a doggie bed in the corner and is already sound asleep, her little snoring noises alternating between various assorted grunts and woofs and growls as she chases something in her dreams. Which isn't all that bad an idea, when you think about it. Chasing things in your dreams. 'Cause those things you pursue in your dreams can't turn around and kill you.

I find another doggie bed, and as soft as it is, I just can't manage to fall asleep, the crazy scenes from two weeks ago keep flashing through my head like it was all just yesterday. And one scene in particular keeps haunting me. That look on Kitn's face as the missile slammed into his car and exploded, so much like the look he gave us at Macy's and Victoria Station, just before he disappeared. And I can't help but remember that the police never found one trace of his body in the wreckage. I shake my head to try and let go of that thought for good. Surely he's dead. He just got vaporized by all the searing heat from the explosion, is all. But somehow that explanation doesn't leave me with all that much solace. Not even a quantum of solace.

Acknowledgments

This book is the product of my lifelong love of London, England, and every other British township, as well. My wife spent her childhood in London, her father being the head of the IBM office for the entire North Sea region, and we make a pilgrimage back to the city every few years. One of our most fervent dreams is to own a narrowboat there, splitting our time between our family in Texas and our own pied-a-terre to Europe. So of course, little Moose and his best friend Bella had to wind up in jolly old London, at least for a book or two.

Many books in this micro-genre of animal detective stories tend to plow the same hallowed ground over and over, and as a result my objective with this little tale (or is it tail?) was to explore the similarities and differences between the British language and culture and that of we (relatively unsophisticated) North Americans, colonists that we are. I've always heartily admired the British, with their deeply ingrained pluck and courage that easily transcends anything we have ever experienced in Fortress America. I certainly hope that admiration shines through, and to keep me from shoving my Yankee foot deeply down my gullet and showing my true ignorance of our brothers and sisters across the Atlantic, I turned to my independent author friends at ALLi for guidance. Virtually overnight, my knight in shining armor galloped in to protect me from a sin almost as embarrassing as the one time I tried to write a serious love scene (something in retrospect no 60-ish man should ever attempt), attempting to convey an accurate depiction of the original English language from the backwoods mindset of a country boy from the great state of Texas. Kind of like grinding up a fine tenderloin steak to form the basis of a good pot of Texas chili. (With no beans, of course, but then I did say it was "Texas" chili.)

Oliver Tooley ("Olli") was a true Godsend for this project, and without his amazing insights this book would have been a cultural embarrassment that could very likely have set my country's relations with Britain back well over two hundred years. Or roughly to the point where Dolly Madison was racing from a burning not-yet-White House with America's few existing treasures in her arms, not exactly a high point in British-American relations. Back to my main point, as fastidious as I try to be in researching my books, Olli provided extensive corrections and suggestions to the story, particularly in regard to the character Dodger. And I will have to admit I ignored many of his suggestions for making Dodger's dialect more realistic, simply because of my own perceived need to balance the accuracy of that dialect with the readability for my American audience. Colonists that we are.

Once again, this book would be unfit for human, canine or even feline consumption but for the love and attention it received from my amazing editor, Kara Vaught. Her mastery of the (American) English language is second to none, and this book is an excellent testament to that, Moose's creative mangling of that language notwithstanding.

The cover design comes from Cathy Helms at Avalon Graphics, who I would enthusiastically recommend. Not only does she create what I think are fantastic covers with great eyeball appeal, she is also amazingly easy to work with. I gave her some general ideas, expecting to have to go through many, many iterations before she finally got it right, but to my surprise she hit it out of the ballpark right off the bat. If you ever want your book judged in a positive way by its cover, call Ms. Helms. I only wish she could work that same magic on my own personal cover.

Speaking of which, my everlasting thanks to Elizabeth, my greatest cheerleader, my inspiration, my best friend forever, and the keeper of my heart. And the one person who saw through the admittedly auspicious cover to explore the (rather questionable) content buried within. It's been almost 40 years, and I still have her fooled.

Last, but certainly not least, thanks to my real inspiration for this book, a fifteen pound bundle of absolute Aussie terror named Moose. He may be gone but he will never be forgotten. And Heaven will never be the same.

About the Author

R ene Fomby practices criminal defense and civil litigation across the state of Texas. A dedicated member of the State Bar's Pro Bono College, Rene takes on the nail-biting cases that most other lawyers turn away. And his life is all the richer for it.

More importantly, Rene is a winemaker, sailor, private pilot, helicopter dad and loving husband, and is currently owned by three very feisty dogs and countless adorable grand dogs and cats. And now, remarkably, by one brand-new human grandpuppy. (Who doesn't mind all the barking one little bit!)

Other Books by Rene Fomby

Private Eyes

From Russia With Fur

Resumed Innocent

The Chi Rho Conspiracy

New Rome Rising

The Game of War

Made in the USA
Middletown, DE
09 February 2020

84318504R00177